HERO IKOS

AXEL GLASCHER

HEROIKOS

Copyright © 2026 by Axel Glascher

First edition

Published in the United States by Youngsford Publishing©

ISBN: 979-8-9946266-0-3 (paperback)

ISBN: 979-8-9946266-1-0 (eBook)

HERO
IKOS

CHAPTER 1

I SPENT MY childhood summers in Arcadia, a small town in Pennsylvania, just east of Harrisburg. It's a quiet place, nestled in the dense forest of the Susquehanna, and stretches for some distance alongside the Whistana River, which gushes through a narrow gorge and then widens and slows its pace, spreading as the valley opens.

I was six the first time I was dropped off in Arcadia. I remember sitting in the back seat of the car, my teary eyes fixed on the unfamiliar landscape as it rolled by. My parents sat very still with their eyes locked on the road, and a thick silence filled the space between us. It was a long ride.

Eventually, we stopped in front of a house I vaguely remembered. I had been there before for some family reunion. My mother stayed in the car, and my father took me by the hand—his other hand gripped a bulky suitcase that looked awfully heavy—and knocked on the door.

I was somewhat comforted when I saw the smiling faces of my grandparents. Mimi hugged me, and Grandpa Nick ruffled my hair, and for a brief moment, everything felt alright. But then the three of them stepped aside and spoke seriously, as grown-ups do when something's wrong. Nick and Mimi nodded gravely as my father spoke. He looked tired.

When they were done, my father put his hand on my shoulder and explained—as if this would suffice—that he and my mother needed to "figure things out."

"I'll be back for you in a couple of days, Andy," he said, but the huge suitcase standing by the door told me otherwise. "Be a good boy and do what your grandparents say."

The first few days were miserable. I felt lonely and sad, my mind full of concerns I couldn't quite understand. But my grandparents were patient and comforting. Nick told silly jokes —and laughed at them—and Mimi baked chocolate cookies. My distress slowly eased, and I became curious about my new surroundings and eager to explore them. The old house was crowded with fascinating objects—sculptures and paintings, books and clocks. Each room was full of mysterious secrets.

Over the years, I would come to know the house very well. It was a stately, rectangular structure with thick stone walls and evenly spaced grid-paneled windows. It had a red front door and a large square porch. On the south side, facing the backyard and the Whistana Valley, it had an ample wooden deck from which one could see over the trees and all the way to a bluish horizon.

The backyard was huge—about an acre—and stretched downward until it met the forest. When Nick and Mimi bought the house in the 1970s, the slope was so steep it rendered the entire backyard useless, with no place for a firepit or even a picnic table. So Nick spent a whole summer building a series of stone-retaining walls, which he then filled with dirt to form terraced levels, transforming the length of the pitch into a succession of flat surfaces, each connected to the following by stone steps.

That first summer, the backyard became my favorite place to play. I would run up and down the terraces, climb the stone steps, and change course each time I completed a lap, tracing different paths by going up one way and then down another. In those moments, with the warm sun on my face, my troubles became a distant whisper, like the soft murmur of the Whistana River in the valley below.

As I had predicted, my first stay with Nick and Mimi turned out to be longer than my father had promised. It would be my mother, in fact, who would pick me up three weeks later and take me back home to the suburbs of Philadelphia. It was good to be back, and yet the house felt strange and empty. My father had left, and with him, a sense of structure had disappeared. All my needs were taken care of, but life felt incomplete and deficient, like a wobbly cart.

My father, George Romano, is the only child of Nick and Mimi and was a teacher, just like they were. He grew up in Arcadia and moved to Philadelphia as soon as he finished college. When he and my mother divorced, he bought an old brick twin in a town called Bradwick, close enough to where we lived so I could visit on the weekends.

My mother, Margaret, was a corporate lawyer. She was the chief legal officer at Brookstone Group, one of those investment trusts for real estate development. She spent long hours at the office and would continue to work late into the night from home. Well past my bedtime, I could still hear her on the phone, snapping orders and talking briskly.

Her crazy schedule was part of the reason I spent so much time in Arcadia. She had so much work she simply couldn't have a kid loafing around the house during the summer. So, as soon as the school year was over, she would pack my stuff and drive me straight to Nick and Mimi's. Apparently, she and my father—and Nick and Mimi, of course—had agreed to that plan. The arrangement definitely worked for me. I had come to love the place.

I would play in the terraced yard and explore the woods beyond, sometimes venturing down the trail all the way to the river. In the afternoons, Nick and Mimi would take me into town to Bernie's Ice Cream Shop—their strawberry was to die for—and then we would cross the street to the park, where I would play with a few other kids about my age.

In the late afternoons, when we were back at the house and the sun had made its way behind the tree line, Nick would sit on his deck chair and tell me the stories of the Greek heroes, the ones we've all heard of at some point in our lives: Theseus, Achilles, Perseus, and so on. Nick had been a history and literature teacher at Central Beaufort in Harrisburg. He also taught classical studies at the Cooper Arts Center and was considered an expert in his field. Many of his papers had been published and were often cited in academic works.

As you would expect from a teacher of the classics, he read a lot. There were books all over the house, which he would leave open, face down, ready to be picked up again at any moment. Their pages were full of scribbling, highlighting, and underlining and crammed with sticky notes peeking out from the sides. He would read about anything and everything, but he had a special interest in ancient literature, philosophy, and religion. Above all else, he was passionate—almost to the point of obsession—about the ancient Greeks.

Thanks to Nick, I developed a fascination for Achilles.

One day, I was staring down in wonder at my feet, snugly fit into the shiny blue running shoes I had seen on TV and begged my mother to buy, when an idea struck me. I was convinced beyond any doubt that those shoes would make me run faster and decided to put them to the test. Nick agreed to help me.

Standing at the bottom of the yard, I took a deep breath through my nose, allowing the warm, perfumed air to fill my tiny lungs, and repeated this several times until I was a bit dizzy. In front of me was one of the flights of stone steps, the lowest one, close to the forest. Two more flights of steps lay ahead of that one, leading all the way up to the house.

"Are you ready, Andy? Go!" Nick's voice called from above.

I dashed forward, determined. I could feel a huge smile contorting my face as I scrambled up the steps, almost tripping over my eager feet as I crossed the first terrace. Then the next flight of steps. And the next.

When I reached the top, I touched one of the fence posts of the garden, my little chest heaving, and instinctively raised both arms in a sign of victory.

"So?" I asked with difficulty as I wiped beads of sweat from my forehead. "Am I faster than Achilles?"

Nick frowned and nodded. "According to my watch, yes, Andy, you are faster than Achilles."

Then Nick said something I can't fully recall, something about "stages" and a "story." He said this as he pointed at the stone steps and the ascending terraces, starting from the bottom of the hill and tracing a line with his finger, all the way to the top. He used the word *hero* as well.... But that's all I can remember.

Nick and I would talk about the Greek heroes every day. He told me their stories, but he also told me what he thought those stories meant, as if they contained some sort of lesson. I heard them so many times, in fact, that I could remember every single detail by heart.

When I was about thirteen, my mother married a guy called Don Slater. I don't have much to say about him one way or the other. I don't see much of him anyway. What is noteworthy is that soon after, the three of us moved to Chicago.

I could no longer spend the weekends with my father in Bradwick, and over time our relationship became estranged, not that it had been great up to that point. At first, we would talk on the phone and I would go through the motions, answering his questions with little enthusiasm. As time went by, those contacts became less frequent, more formal and to the point. When he called, I was not always available, and when I was, I was aloof or in a rush.

I knew even at the time that he meant well. I could hear it in his voice, which was soft and kind and supportive. But that didn't stop me from holding a bit of a grudge on him. Part of me was still angry that he had divorced my mother and left me when I was a kid, that he had packed that huge suitcase and told me he would pick me up "in a few days."

Moving to Chicago also meant I would no longer

spend my summers in Arcadia. It was too far away. Too inconvenient. I stayed in touch with Nick and Mimi, of course, and I even spent a Thanksgiving week with them when I was about fifteen. But, inevitably, distance did its work and our interactions became less frequent. Time went by, as it does when we are busy with the little dramas of our present, and, one birthday after another, my teenage years came and went, full of things that now seem unimportant.

At one point, Mimi fell ill. She had kidney cancer. It was bad; I knew that much. But the details of her situation were fuzzy, in part because my father wouldn't provide a whole lot of information. I suppose I was still a kid in his eyes and he wanted to spare me the horrors of disease.

But I didn't inquire too much about her health either. I simply went about my own business, pushing the thought of Mimi and her suffering to one side. Maybe it was my own way of dealing with it. Maybe it was simply a case of the young being too preoccupied with their own future to be bothered by those who had none left. I don't know… But I feel guilty about it. I should have been closer to her, more involved.

It was Mimi for heaven's sake.

One day my father called to tell me she had died.

"She is at peace now," he said. "She's in a better place."

I knew what he meant, but I was still a bit bugged at him for saying that. *How can she be in a better place? And how could you know anything about it?* I thought. *No, she is not in a better place. She is nowhere. She's dead.*

When we hung up, I cried. I was sad. But I was also angry. About what or with whom, I couldn't tell.

❧

The reason we moved to Chicago had nothing to do with my mother marrying Don. It was all about work. And money.

She had left her corporate job and, using her extensive network and influences, had brokered a leveraged buyout of a Chicago-based realty firm. It was one of those nameless, faceless companies no one knows about but nonetheless moves hefty sums of money every year. It specialized in funding and developing urban infrastructure: apartment buildings, office campuses, and shopping malls. As its sole owner, my mother renamed it "Grimshaw Realty." (Grimshaw is her maiden name.)

In just a few short years and under my mother's fierce leadership, Grimshaw Realty had tripled the amount of building contracts in its portfolio and had exponentially grown its stakes in private equity ventures. My mother had shoved competitors out of the way and muscled new terms on her vendors. Government officials, bankers, and even her own board of governors were terrified of her and would nod in submission under her sharp gaze.

Soon, the company became one of the big players at a national level with sizable operations in the Midwest and Northeast. As its dominion grew, Grimshaw Realty came to be known simply as "Grimshaw," and one was never sure if people were talking about the company or about my mother.

It was a vast kingdom, which she ruled over as a harsh queen. And I, Andy Romano, was to be her successor, groomed and taught and trained every single day.

CHAPTER 2

I HAD JUST turned twenty-one and was wrapping up my junior year at Lindenfield College, where I was majoring in business. Spring was in the air; faces were smiling and everything looked bright. "Move-out day" had arrived, the time to empty our dorms and return home for the summer.

I would be heading back to Chicago later in the afternoon, so I had plenty of time to kill, watching the parade of movers as I waited. I had been looking forward to this day for a while, and not only because it meant the end of the academic cycle. As soon as the first student was out the door, the whole atmosphere at Lindenfield would relax, leading to all sorts of shenanigans and disorderly behavior. Move-out day could be quite an entertaining affair.

But move-out day was also exciting in subtler ways. There was a special atmosphere, something like electricity in the air, a promise of adventure and change. Moving out was a threshold of sorts, a marker in time that allowed us to appreciate our own growth and personal progress. We would return home transformed after a full school year. And when we all met again in the fall, we would be further changed by our experiences during the summer.

That was especially true in my case.

My mother had arranged an intensive training program for me at Grimshaw. Starting immediately once I was back in Chicago, I would be working there as an intern, taking part in a full rotational program lasting all summer. She was preparing me, training me to become a manager and, eventually, her successor as CEO.

I was the heir to the Grimshaw throne, and I was eager to get going and claim my birthright. Mother was eager too, in her own way, and she would push me along, setting ambitious targets, adding new assignments, and urging me to take on responsibilities that were often beyond my capabilities and experience.

The internship she had arranged for me that summer was a clear example. I would spend roughly three weeks in each of four different roles. Starting as urban planning assistant, my job would be to learn about community impact, zoning regulations, and environmental compliance. I would also fill the shoes of a financial analyst intern, a project coordinator, and a construction management intern.

Mother had also secured a spot for me at the annual meeting of the Midwest Chapter of the Land and Property Society, which was huge—and literally unprecedented—for a student like me. I would be sharing a table with members of the Chicago Real Estate Board, city planners, infrastructure advisers, and private equity managers.

In one of her many text messages—which she sent constantly when she wanted my attention—Mother explained that it had not been easy to secure a spot for me at the conference, that she'd had to twist a few arms before the organizers yielded. The funny thing is that I couldn't quite tell if she was speaking figuratively or if she had actually *twisted their arms.*

All this was typical of her. It was an audacious—and maybe even an unreasonable—plan, and as much as I was excited, I was also somewhat apprehensive. It all felt a bit too soon and a bit too much, and I wondered whether I would feel out of place, surrounded by others with much more experience and seniority. *Would they take me seriously or just put up with me?* I could almost imagine the people whispering to one another: "That's Grimshaw's kid. You better treat him well or she will *twist your arm.*"

Of all the places one could get a good view of the movers, the study lounge in Rochester Dormitory was probably the best. I took a seat at my favorite spot, a secluded booth at the far end of the room, nestled against the large window-pane that ran across the front of the building. From there, I could see a good stretch of both sidewalks of Lindenfield Street, which was the main road leading to the parking lot.

A crowd of students marched up and down the road, each going about their business. Some were walking toward the parking lot, pushing carts and carrying things in their arms. Others were returning empty-handed to load more stuff from their dorms.

Every few minutes, my phone would buzz with messages from Mother, all containing instructions and logistical details about my internship. She also explained she would be traveling to California the following week to meet some "private equity people." I was expected at the office on Monday, where I would be put through a series of drills and preps for the big conference in June.

"Andy," read the last of her texts, "we need at least three weeks to prep you for the Midwest meeting. You need a full background and a 'who's who.' The sooner we start, the better. Stay focused!"

After a long silence, the phone buzzed again.

"Dear Andy," read the new message, "this is your grandfather. How are you? If it's not too much of an inconvenience and when you have a moment, I would appreciate if you gave me a call. With kind regards, Nicholas Romano."

I smiled. The way he wrote the text was endearing, and its polite formality was almost heartbreaking. It had been a while since I'd talked to him, and my shoulders felt heavy with guilt, as if I had betrayed some noble principle.

I pressed "call back" and took a deep breath, unsure how the conversation would go.

"Hello," said an older voice.

"Hey, Nick," I said. I had always called him Nick for some reason. "How are you? It's Andy."

"Well, hello, young man! My dear, dear Andy." His voice cracked, and he cleared his throat. "I can't tell you how happy I am to hear your voice. How are you?"

We talked for a bit, enough to exchange basic updates. Nick asked about my health and about my mother and Don and our life in Chicago. He wanted to know about my studies and whether I had a girlfriend or not. All the things grandparents go on and on about.

Then, he changed the subject.

"Look, Andy," he said, "I'll get to the point, because you probably have a lot to do. I..." He became hesitant and a bit awkward. "When Mimi got sick, I started neglecting the yard. I didn't have the time—or the energy, I suppose—to work on it. My mind was somewhere else. I was worried about Mimi. One week turned into another, and the months went by and… well… what I'm trying to say is that since Mimi left us I haven't… I suppose I haven't been my usual self.

"The point is that the yard is a mess. The overgrowth has gotten a bit out of control. Weeds, grasses, vines, thistles. You know? I thought, well, now that you must be closing out your school year and getting ready for the summer, maybe you could spend a week or so with me in Arcadia and we could both work on the yard. It would be nice to have you here, just like old times."

"You want me to come to Arcadia and do yard work with you?" I repeated slowly, just to make sure I had heard correctly. I had never done a day of yard work in my life, and I knew absolutely nothing about it. Of all the possible ways in which I could help Nick, this was probably the one I was least qualified for.

"Yes. That's it," confirmed Nick.

"But…" I was still trying to organize my thoughts. "Can't you hire a landscaping service?"

"I am afraid, dear Andy, that things are a bit more complicated.… It's a rather long story."

Silence followed. It was my turn to speak, but I wasn't sure what to say.

This doesn't sound at all like Nick was my first thought. *But what do I know? I haven't had a meaningful conversation with him in… how long? Since Mimi died, and that was about two years ago. All our interactions have been brief and to the point. Happy birthday. Merry Christmas. Happy New Year. But not much more.*

"Hello?" said Nick.

"Yes, I'm here," I said, but I was still thinking. *Nick isn't telling me the whole story. Something doesn't feel right. But… what difference does that make? I have to get back to Chicago and show up sharp and ready at Grimshaw on Monday morning.*

"I would love to help you, Nick," I said. "I mean it. And I would love to spend some time with you in Arcadia. But I have this big conference coming up, and my internship in Mom's company starts on Monday. It's a big opportunity for me."

"In that case," said Nick, sounding cheerful again, "you must go. The grievances of the old should not interfere with the plans of the young. That's something like a cosmic law." He chuckled. "And besides, I'll figure something out. It's just some vines and general overgrowth. Nothing an expert gardener like myself can't deal with."

We said our goodbyes and I just sat there, staring out the window.

CHAPTER 3

THE STUDY LOUNGE was in complete silence as I sat there, my eyes still fixed on the busy sidewalk, looking at nothing. Then I found myself walking up Lindenfield Street, occasionally stepping aside to prevent a collision with a bucket cart or a student carrying boxes. When I left Rochester Hall behind me, I made the first left and crossed the park toward Wayne Auditorium. It was less crowded there, and I had no trouble finding a bench in the shade.

I was seized by a strange feeling, a thought I couldn't quite articulate. It made my temples throb and blocked out all my internal chatter, leaving behind an annoying white noise. It took me a while to shake the feeling off and, as soon as I did, memories of Arcadia began to parade in front of me, one after the next, stitched together like patchwork.

I remembered the stone steps in Nick and Mimi's yard, each flight connecting one terrace to the next. The steps were flanked by thick flower shrubs, and I heard Nick call them "azaleas" in a distant, muffled voice.

I was retrieving memories I didn't even know I possessed. I remembered, for example, a hilly landscape and a grand mansion surrounded by trees. I was standing in the courtyard, playing with other children. We were eating pastries and running around. Then I saw Grandpa Nick sitting in one of his deck chairs, telling me the story of the great Achilles.

I began to wonder about Nick's situation, how he was all alone since Mimi had died. *How did he manage the silence day after day in that house full of memories? Did he go into town at all to have an ice cream at Bernie's, or to the park to talk to people or pet a dog? Maybe that's what Nick had called me for*, I thought. *Maybe he was just feeling lonely.* Helping him with the yard sounded like some silly excuse to get me over there and spend some time together.

This seemed like a perfectly reasonable explanation, and yet something about our conversation didn't quite add up. And when I suggested a landscaping company, he had said that things were a bit more "complicated."

There must be something else, I thought, *but he probably won't tell me if I ask.*

If I called him again to inquire further, he would simply wave the whole thing away, not wanting to burden me with his troubles. He would insist I focus on my future and minimize his own needs to make me feel better. If I really wanted to get to the bottom of the whole thing, I would have to call my father; he was the only one who would know something about Nick's situation.

I browsed my contacts until I found "George Romano" but paused before going any further. I wasn't too keen on talking to him.

Maybe we could text, I thought. *No. He'll just call me back as soon as he sees my message. I'll just have to call him.*

❦

"What a nice surprise, Andy!" said my father after a moment of bewildered confusion. "It's so nice of you to call. How are you? You must be getting ready for move-out day, aren't you? How did your finals go?"

He had a bunch of questions like that and was genuinely interested in small details and basic updates, all of which seemed trifling and inconsequential. I answered politely but briefly and eventually was able to steer the conversation toward my call with Nick.

"Yeah…" he groaned. "I'm a bit worried about Dad myself."

"He said something about his yard being a mess, which doesn't make any sense," I said.

"Since Mom… Since Mimi got sick, things have been tough for Nick. I think the house has become too big for him. It's just too much for him to manage. I mean, perhaps keeping the house in order is not so much the issue. But maintaining that yard is another story altogether."

I was beginning to lose my patience with him. He wasn't a practical person, and his thought process wasn't solution oriented.

"Can't we just hire a landscaping company to fix whatever the issue is? It can't be that complicated," I said.

"Listen, Andy, you haven't seen Arcadia in several years. There's not a whole lot of businesses operating in town. The kids that mow the lawn during the summer don't have the equipment to deal with Dad's yard. We also looked into a landscaping service from Glendale and eventually found a guy who agreed to drive all the way to Arcadia. But when he saw the state the yard was in and all the quirky terraces and stone steps…"

"What?" I urged.

"Well, let's just say he wasn't too happy with the deal. He said driving all the way to Arcadia for one yard was bad business for him, unless we signed an annual contract for a full landscaping service. He quoted a ridiculous price."

"If it's a matter of money…" I said.

"It's not about the money, Andy. You sound like your mother, for heaven's sake. The landscaping service is not even the point. The point is that Dad is all alone up there. Maybe it's time for him to move to a smaller place, closer to Bradwick, where I can see him more regularly, take better care of him. As things stand today, I can only see him so often."

"But he loves that house!" I protested, even though I sensed he was right. "That house is his life."

"I know, I know. But there's not much we can do."

My mother would never say something like that. In fact, she would likely bang her fist on the table and say that nothing was impossible. *How could the two of them be so different?*

"Then there's the issue with the township," he continued. "There's a statute that requires neighbors to keep their lawns properly mowed and the shrubbery under control. Otherwise, there are pest-control issues and something about invasive species of vines spreading around. Dad's already been fined by the township, and things will only get worse over time.

"Our old neighbor, Mr. Snopengaard—you might remember him from when you spent your summers there— is the township manager. He's a good man. He reached out to me not long ago and expressed his concern about Dad. He seemed really worried."

I remained silent. He had a point, and I couldn't deny it. At the same time, something told me Nick still had a few more good years in that house before he moved. What he needed was help, someone to lean on.

"There must be something we can do," I said with an edge in my voice. "You can't force Nick to move out."

My father sighed.

"Of course I can't, Andy. But Dad needs to be reasonable. It's time for him to move, to close this chapter in his life. I'll drive to Arcadia in a few weeks and try to talk some sense into him. Look… this is for his own good."

We hung up and I sighed, watching the passersby as they carried their belongings. The sun was high, and the shade from the trees had shrunk to small circles, like little islands in an ocean of pavers. I shook my head. It was always the same story with my father: our conversations never led to solutions, and far from bringing us together, they somehow made us even more estranged.

My heart was heavy as I walked back to my dorm. All things came to an end eventually; I could understand that. But before they did, they existed as lesser versions of themselves. Nick and Mimi's backyard would become derelict and overgrown. Their happy household in Arcadia would become dim and quiet. The smell of Mimi's cookies would fade. And a smart and confident Nick would end up calling his grandson for help, maybe as a last resort.

If my father was right—and I was afraid, somewhere deep inside, that he just might be—Nick would have to leave behind the house he loved so much. The house he'd put so much effort and care into.

It didn't seem fair.

By the time I reached Lindenfield Street, a new thought possessed me. I picked up pace, and my hands knotted into fists. Nick and Mimi had been there for me when my parents split. They had comforted me during those difficult days when my little world was falling apart. They had soothed my terrified heart and had been patient with my tantrums. They had, slowly but inexorably, replaced my childhood pain with laughter and fun and bewilderment.

Mimi is dead, I thought, *and I should have been there for her. Now I must be there for Nick. I must go to Arcadia. I must!*

But just as my resolve was reaching its peak, doubt and fear sneaked in.

What about my internship? After all the preparations and plans. Mother will kill me. Forget about twisted arms. She-will-actually-kill-me.

"Unless…" I said out loud. "Unless I postpone the start of my internship by just a couple of weeks."

It was by no means a perfect plan. My summer schedule was insanely ambitious as things stood. If I shaved off two weeks from the program, it would be impossible to get through the whole thing before the end of summer. And on top of it, the Land and Property Conference was scheduled for mid-June, and I needed the drills if I wanted to be fully prepared. It was, no matter how much I turned it over in my mind, a bad idea. And my mother would have nothing of it, that was for sure.

But it was the only solution I could think of.

I had to give it a try.

⁋

"Yes," she said over the speaker. Her voice was sharp and commanding.

"Hi, Mom." I tried to sound casual, but I wasn't convincing. There was a moment of silence.

"Is everything alright?"

I coughed and cleared my throat.

"Yes, yes, everything's good. I got all the information you sent. Yes."

I had to clear my throat again.

"Well?" she said after another moment of silence.

"Please don't get mad but… I… there's…"

"There's what? Speak up and say what you need to say. I'm busy."

My blood boiled for a moment, causing my face to flush, warming my forehead, and making my lips and cheeks throb.

"Well?"

"I… there's something… something's come up. I need a few days before I return to Chicago," I stuttered.

An icy silence fell between us.

"What can possibly be more important than your internship? It doesn't sound like you're taking this seriously."

I swallowed, but my mouth was dry. Then I took a deep breath and found—from where I am not sure—some determination.

"Grandpa Nick needs my help. It's only for a couple of weeks. Then I'll—"

"What does the old man want?" she interrupted. She was still annoyed, but there was a hint of curiosity in her voice. I was about to answer when I was struck with just how unfair it was for her to talk about Nick with such disdain. *Hadn't she dropped me off at his house and left me in his care for six summers in a row? It had certainly been convenient for her at the time.*

"Well?!"

My blood boiled again, and this time it was enough to thaw my spine. The words finally came out as I intended.

"Something's wrong with him, and he needs my help. It'll only be two weeks. This is something I must do."

"What about your father? This sounds like something he should take care of."

I had been waiting for her to bring my father into the conversation. It was time to play my first card.

"No. You know how that is. He's not a problem solver. He's not like you and me."

I paused to let the statement sink in. Then I continued.

"The conference is in late June. I can be in Chicago by the end of May, and there would still be plenty of time for me to get ready. Then I can stay on for the internship until the end of August. Besides"—this was my second card, so I paused again—"I can take some material with me to Arcadia and study while I'm there. I'll schedule time for reading every night. I am a fast learner, Mom."

"I know you are, Andy, and that's exactly why we need to take full advantage of your summer."

"Look, Mom, I wouldn't bring this up if I didn't think it was important. Please understand."

There was another long silence.

"It sounds like you're asking for my permission, Andy, but this is entirely up to you. You're a man now, and your choices are yours and yours alone. I must remind you, however, that your choices are a reflection of your priorities, and conflicting priorities are a bad thing."

Her tone became hard again.

"Listen to me carefully because this is important. Managing a company like ours requires complete dedication, full commitment. You may be smart. You may be a fast learner. But if you want to run Grimshaw someday, you'll have to show me that you are capable of putting your responsibilities above everything else. That means making sacrifices, saying goodbyes, and never looking back. It's the only way."

"It's only two weeks, Mom. I'll be in the office Monday morning two weeks from now. I promise."

"As I said, it's your choice. Send my regards to Nicholas. Oh, and don't let the old man put funny ideas in your head. He does that. You've been warned."

She hung up.

CHAPTER 4

THE ARCADIA TRAIN station stood right off the turn-pike and had been abandoned since the 1980s. Its hall and platform still stood, but the walls had turned dark with grime and the signs near the main entrance had faded. Above the platform, the corrugated metal roof had corroded and the ironwork of the canopy had rusted to a bright orange.

The tracks, ironically, were still busy. Passenger lines—connecting Harrisburg to New York and Pittsburgh—would rush by every now and then without stopping. Freight trains would rumble through as well, although less frequently, moving their loads in mile-long formations.

The only way to get to Arcadia was by long-distance bus, which would stop at the train station's parking lot, a bleak patch of asphalt with weeds growing through its cracks.

"This stop is Arcadia. Arcadia, everybody. If this is your stop, please take a moment to collect your belong-ings. Watch your step as you descend. Once again, this is Arcadia," said the driver into the sound system as he rolled onto the uneven pavement of the parking lot.

I was tired and sore. I had flown out of O'Hare in the

early morning and taken the first Pittsburgh-bound bus from Philadelphia International. I had spent most of my day cramped into some unnatural position and was happy to hop off and stretch my arms and legs.

Good to see you again, Arcadia, I thought as I looked around.

I had assumed I would be the only passenger stopping at Arcadia, so I was surprised when a tall girl stepped off the bus right behind me. She pulled the luggage compartment open, grabbed a small suitcase, and then leaned toward the door and exchanged a few words with the driver. They seemed to know each other. I couldn't quite hear what they said over the idling diesel engine, but after a brief moment, she laughed heartily and waved goodbye.

She dragged her suitcase to the steps of the station hall, found a spot to sit, and bent over her phone. She had ash-blond hair and wore faded jeans and a white top. I tried to see her face, but her wavy hair tumbled past her shoulders and covered it from view.

I didn't mean to gape, but I became curious and wanted to see what she looked like, so I let my eyes linger for a moment, just long enough to catch a glimpse of her as she tucked a tress behind her ear. She had an elegant face, high cheekbones, a well-defined jawline, and a strong nose.

She looked up at me all of a sudden as if she'd known I was watching, and I instinctively turned away, embarrassed I'd been caught. I shuffled my feet and looked around, finally fixing my attention on the train platform.

"Are you sure this is where you're supposed to be?" she asked.

Her voice was loud and clear and projected with ease over the hum of the turnpike traffic. It was an honest question, but there was something playful in her tone, a hint of mischief.

"This is New York City, right?" I said, looking around and pretending to be confused.

She laughed. It was the same laugh I'd heard when she waved goodbye to the bus driver: wide, hearty, and unabashed.

I smiled and kicked some loose gravel. I was glad she'd liked my joke. But soon I was overtaken by a rather somber feeling. Her question had stirred something in my mind, and I found myself thinking about it.

Is this really where I'm supposed to be?

I was supposed to be in Chicago, not in some forsaken parking lot in the middle of nowhere. I had traveled far and veered off course, driven by old memories, a splash of guilt, and a vague desire to make up for old mistakes.

"Hello?" The girl's voice snapped me out of my thoughts.

"Sorry," I said.

"You sort of… spaced out for a moment."

"Yes, I guess I do that sometimes."

She rolled her eyes.

"But seriously, where are you heading? Getting a ride in these parts won't be easy."

"No kidding," I said, looking down at my phone. I didn't want to disturb Nick, so I had tried several times to schedule a ride, but all my requests had timed out. There were no drivers available.

"If you're heading into town, we can give you a ride. My dad is on his way to pick me up."

"Actually," I said, "I'm going past the town center, all the way to the end of Arcadia, to Laurel Hill."

She squinted and gave me a long suspicious look.

"Do you know anyone up there?" she asked. She spoke slowly as if she knew the answer to her own question.

"Yes. My grandfather. Nicholas Romano."

"You've got to be kidding me," she gasped. "It *is* you. I somehow knew it, but my brain kept telling me it was impossible."

I smiled politely while my mind raced in a frantic attempt to remember.

"I'm Sally," she said, shaking her head in disbelief.

I stared at her blankly.

"Sally Higgins, you numb nuts!"

Then it all hit me.

Strawberry ice cream.

Giggles.

Pigtails.

"Sally Higgins…" I said in a daze. "We had ice cream at your dad's shop almost every afternoon. We played in the park…"

Nick and Mimi would take me into town every afternoon, and we would always stop at Bernie's Ice Cream Shop. In fact, during the summer, there was no "going into town" without a stop at Bernie's. Neighbors, and even people from out of town, would flock to his store just for a taste of his homemade and carefully crafted custards and ice creams.

I also remembered the park across the street. There was a little gang of us—maybe four or five kids—and we would play together. I could remember Sally very clearly; she was a funny girl with freckles and braces, her hair tied into pigtails.

"You're so…" I mumbled. "You've changed."

At that moment, looking straight at her, I realized just how pretty she was, and I was struck dumb and couldn't think of anything else to say.

A car rolled slowly toward us, crunching gravel and loose asphalt under its wheels.

"Come on, numb nuts. We'll give you a ride," said Sally.

She introduced me to her father, but there was no need. I knew who he was. I had heard the story from Mimi, and I remembered it, just as I'd remembered Sally and her pigtails. Bernard Higgins Jr. was the proprietor of Bernie's Ice Cream Shop and the eldest son of its founder, Mr. Bernard Higgins Sr., known to everyone as "Bernie."

He knew who I was too. He asked about my father, whom he had been close with for most of his young life. He said some kind words about Mimi, about how she was missed and all that. Finally, he asked about Mother, which surprised me. He said he'd seen her on the news talking about some development in the Midwest.

I answered all his questions politely but briefly.

"I'll drive you to Laurel Hill, if you like," he said.

"Thank you. I appreciate it," I said and sat in the back seat.

"So, what brings you to Arcadia, young Romano? Any grand plans?" asked Higgins as we drove out of the parking lot.

"I'll just be staying with Nick for a couple of weeks. To keep him company."

"That's very decent of you," he said, nodding at me through the mirror. He had bushy eyebrows and a firm expression, the look of someone you wouldn't want to mess with. "I've seen Nicholas in town a few times, but he always seems to be going somewhere. I haven't had a chance to talk to him in a while. He'll be happy to see you."

From the train station, the car made its way onto the main road, which connected the turnpike to Arcadia's main square. It was a slightly curved strip of pavement, flanked on both sides by abandoned factories, dormant beasts of rust, each with a faded sign that gave it a name, like headstones in a giant cemetery: Bethlehem Steel, Dauphin Cotton Factory, Armstrong Cork Company, and so on.

Most of them had large brick facades, stone trim, and decorative cornices, signs of better times and optimistic grandeur. Yet one had to look hard to see past the decay and disrepair. Most of the corbels had crumbled beyond recognition, and the mortar between the bricks had been eaten away by rain and frost. In some of them, entire sections of brick wall had collapsed into heaps of rubble.

One after the next, they stretched out as far as I could see.

"Isn't it sad?" asked Sally. "All this?"

"Hmm," I said, staring at the buildings as we passed them.

Arcadia had enjoyed a period of splendor, back in the time when factories in the region operated double shifts, sending their produce along the Eastern Division Canal and the Pennsylvania Railroad. The town expanded during those glorious decades, giving rise to stylish buildings and stately homes.

But when the factories closed, everyone left. They moved to Pittsburgh, Philadelphia, and Harrisburg, and some even took off to other states. The streets grew quiet, many stores were boarded up, and the factories along the main road were left to rust and crumble. Arcadia's charm dwindled until it became a shadow of its former self.

"I wish they would just knock them down and, I don't know… plant some trees instead."

"Hmm," I said again.

"We've tried, you know." She turned around in her seat, facing me. "Through the township authorities."

She was really beautiful.

"What?"

"I said that we've tried to get the holding companies to take responsibility and do the right thing. But it all seems useless. Nobody cares."

"Yeah, good luck with that. They'll never take them down," I said, and I looked out the window again.

I knew it was almost impossible to get those buildings knocked down. I knew it very well, in fact. I had studied the whole thing in depth. Well, to be more precise, Mother had told me countless times about "asset abandonment" and its legal ramifications. It was an important aspect of Grimshaw's business, and she made sure I learned the whole thing, inside and out.

"Companies do this all the time," I said distractedly, still looking at the parade of ruins. "They abandon properties in areas where real estate values are declining."

"Why? Why would they do that?" asked Sally.

"Well," I started, repeating what I knew, "if the resale value of the land justifies demolition, they might do it, but in a place like Arcadia, that's unlikely."

Higgins and Sally were both silent, so I continued.

"The thing is, if the factory is abandoned—provided it's 'legitimate abandonment'—the company gets to write off the remaining book value of the building as a loss, which can be a chunky tax benefit if the property hasn't fully depreciated. Abandoning the building also avoids demolition costs, which are deductible, of course, but they usually complicate accounting. Besides—and this is a big risk nowadays—tearing these buildings down is likely to expose environmental hazards, which are a huge headache. So yes, basically, it's better to just leave them like that. You know, just stay away from the mess. Avoid the liability."

I looked at them and shrugged.

There was a long silence, and I thought I saw them exchange glances.

"That sounds like smart talk for a fancy boardroom," said Higgins. "A bunch of executives in nice ties patting themselves on the shoulder and laughing at how clever they are. But this"—he waved at the road ahead—"this is a huge travesty, a corporate abomination. It's indecent, that's what it is." He turned around and looked me straight in the eye. "You know, fancy talk like that is what makes the world an ugly place."

"Dad…" said Sally.

His reaction caught me completely off guard, and it took me a moment to realize I had said something I shouldn't have. Those abandoned factories were a stark reminder of something, perhaps of the good times that were lost forever. And besides, Higgins was right. I felt the same way about the whole thing. Asset abandonment could look good on paper or sound like a smart call in a corporate meeting, but that didn't make it a good thing. And yes, it certainly made the world an ugly place.

"I didn't mean to imply it was a good thing," I tried to explain. "I was just pointing out how companies make these decisions. But you're right. It's a horrible thing to do."

Higgins clicked his tongue and stared at the road.

❧

The town center was just as quaint and charming as I remembered. The main street was spotless and lined with brick Victorian houses and some shops and diners on each side. Some old stores were boarded up, the same ones that had been closed for decades. One was a square building with a faded sign that read *Arcadia General Emporium*. A few shops down was a smaller building, which had also been closed forever: the Arcadia Mercantile Co.

The main square was a little park with walkways and benches and centennial trees. Around it stood a church made of gray stone blocks, a gas station, a bank, and the post office. A large, dignified building towered opposite the church. The words *Township of Arcadia* were carved into the stone above the main entrance.

"That's where I work," said Sally, pointing. "It's the township building. Whenever I'm back from school, I work in administration. Nothing fancy. Forms and permits, that kind of thing."

She smiled as she said this and looked up at the building as we passed. Then she turned toward me again.

"There's just a few of us in the office, so we all do a bit of everything, but I work mostly for Mr. Snopengaard. Summers are the busiest. We have to catch up with all the filing and set ourselves up for property tax collection in the fall."

"Mr. Snopengaard," I repeated slowly. It was a strange name, and it rang a bell.

"Karl Snopengaard," said Sally. "He's the township manager. Well, he's also the treasurer and the solicitor. He practically runs Arcadia."

I remembered at once. He was that neighbor my father had told me about, the one who was concerned about Nick.

We reached the main intersection and took the road to Laurel Hill, a residential neighborhood hidden in the woodland on the west side of Arcadia. The road meandered the hilly landscape, and for a short distance, we could see the Whistana River as it rushed along, splashing against boulders at times and collecting in small pools at others. We were in a different world all of a sudden.

Laurel Hill had been the lifeline of Arcadia when the factories shut down. Besides its natural beauty and elegant houses, it was relatively close to Harrisburg, so it became a viable option for a few brave commuters, those willing to drive in the opposite direction and all the way through town before reaching the highway.

When my grandparents saw Laurel Hill for the first time in the late 1970s, they fell in love with it. It was charming and convenient and cheaper than other suburbs like Elizabethville and Midport, which meant they could afford a larger house.

Toward the end of the road, the woodland opened up to the right, revealing several acres of sloping pastures enclosed by a wooden rail fence that ran all the way to the horizon. On the top of the hill stood an imposing manor. The whole scene was breathtaking.

"That's the Collinsworth Estate," said Higgins, pointing at the house on the hill. "Although no one's seen Greg Collinsworth in years. I believe he lives in New York now. He and your grandfather used to be good friends."

The road came to an end, and the car turned left onto a short lane with a generous cul-de-sac at its end. That was the very last portion of Arcadia, and there were no more roads beyond it.

There were only two houses on the left side of the lane—if one was driving off the main road, that is. Nick and Mimi's house was the one at the very end, its driveway running straight onto the cul-de-sac. On the opposite side, the farmland we'd seen before extended all the way to the next hill.

As the car slowed down, I was able to see the house in more detail. The front yard looked just as abandoned as the factories we'd passed earlier. The grass had grown knee-high, and clusters of thistles had sprung up here and there.

"Are you sure Nicholas is okay?" asked Higgins as he looked around. There was concern in his eyes.

"Yes, he's fine," I said, trying to sound confident. "Thanks for the ride."

"Come into town one day," said Sally. "I'll treat you to some ice cream."

We exchanged our contact information and I waved goodbye as the car drove off.

I stood there for a moment. Everything was still and quiet, and the silence made me uneasy. I decided to take a better look before I knocked and made my way around the house to get a glimpse of the backyard. When I reached the side of the garage, I was shocked to see vines creeping up the wall, forming a thick mat that protruded about two feet. The shrubbery that lined the side of the house had grown to a disproportionate size—almost my height as I passed by.

But the real surprise came when I rounded the next

corner and the backyard came into view. The thing is, there was no backyard, nothing that even resembled one, at least. The entire surface was covered with high grass and thistles, and thickly knit clumps of vines, running all the way down to the edge of the woodland. It was impossible to distinguish the terraces, or see the fire pit, or the raised beds in the vegetable garden, as if a jungle had grown over an ancient city.

CHAPTER 5

NICK'S FACE LIT up when he opened the door, and he chuckled and shook his head. His white hair stood on one side, pressed against his scalp as if he'd just woken from a nap. His beard, always neatly trimmed, appeared patchy and overgrown. He looked older and a bit frail, but his gray eyes were just as I remembered them: steady, curious, and clever.

"It's so good to see you, young man!" he said, looking away for a moment to wipe his tears.

"It's good to see you too, Nick," I managed to say before I choked up.

Then he put his arms around me, gave me a good squeeze, and gently directed me inside, patting my shoulder.

The house was dark and smelled like the windows hadn't been opened in a while. The whole atmosphere, in fact, was rather dreary. Nick didn't seem to notice, as if he'd grown used to it. He sat me on the living room couch and brought some lemonade from the kitchen.

"Tell me about college," he said with wide eyes. "Tell me everything."

"Everything?" I laughed.

"Yes. Everything."

I started with the basics of my life at Lindenfield. I told him about my dorm and my classes and about the many shenanigans my friends and I got up to.

But he was interested in other things, like which classes I found engaging and which ones I didn't. He wanted to know if I had learned something useful for life or that had surprised me. He also asked if I disagreed with anything I had been taught and seemed a bit disappointed when I said I didn't. He never asked about my grades. I noticed this because my grades were always the first thing my mother would ask about.

When we were done with our first round of updates, I took a moment to open the blinds and the windows. Fresh air swept through the room and, almost instantly, the smell of deep forest and fresh grass took over. Daylight shone in as well, chasing away somber thoughts. Nick looked around in surprise and nodded in approval.

"I should've done that a while ago," he said.

It was his turn to speak, and I listened closely as he told me about the last few years. I knew what had happened, of course, but I was only aware of the outline. I was familiar with the facts, but I'd never sat by Nick's side and looked in his eyes as he told his story. They had been difficult years, to say the least. Mimi, he explained, had grown increasingly ill for a few years before she died.

"There were times of despair," said Nick softly, "but there were also times of deep love: love for life and love for one another. There were even times of laughter—you know how Mimi was."

He shrugged.

"All I can say is that we managed to stay together till the end, and I believe that's a good thing."

He went on to explain that after Mimi died, he had been overwhelmed by loneliness.

"Everything was upside down, and I just didn't have the energy to get on top of things again."

For a moment, I considered what my father had said, that it would make more sense for Nick to move somewhere else, closer to Bradwick.

He might be right, I conceded.

"Your dad wants me to move out," said Nick as if he'd read my mind. "I know it's the logical solution, and I know he means well. I'm not senile, you know? I may be a bit stubborn, but I still got my wits about me." He went to the kitchen and returned with two fresh glasses of lemonade.

"But why do you want to stay?" I asked. "Keeping the yard and the house must be a lot of work."

"It's not that bad. Things got out of hand for a bit. That's all."

I gave him a skeptical look.

"When Mimi died… it's hard to explain." He shook his head slowly as he searched for the right words. "It's like I spent the last two years sleepwalking. That's the best I can do to describe it. It took me all this time to snap out of a dark, numb trance."

"I understand," I said and felt a bit silly for saying that. I did understand what he was saying, but I had no idea what it felt like, what they had both gone through.

"Things started slipping, you know? Days turned into weeks and then into months. Just like that. Before I knew it, the yard was a terrible mess. I tried a couple of times to fix it, but I could only work on a bit at a time, and, well, weeds and vines have the bad habit of growing very quickly. I just couldn't keep up.

"Then the warning letters started coming from the township. They threatened me with fines and all sorts of penalties if I didn't take care of the lawn—as if they didn't have anything more important to do.

"It's that good-for-nothing Snopengaard, the township manager. He also happens to be my neighbor up the street, so every time the lawn grew too high, the Snoops would come around and take pictures and give me grief for the state of the yard."

"The Snoops?" I asked.

"Yes. The Snopengaards. Karl and his wife, Irina. Always snooping around. Karl was the one who called up your dad. Can you believe it? He expressed his 'concern' about my condition. Always sticking his snoopy nose into other people's business…"

Nick took a thirsty gulp of his lemonade, draining the glass.

"Anyway"—he slapped his thighs—"Once I get the yard back in shape, it will be easier to maintain. I have a nice tractor mower, you know?"

"So, you were serious about needing my help with the yard," I said.

"Of course I was serious. You are my *soter*." He smiled and then added, "That's what the ancient Greeks called their saviors."

"Well, this *soter*—or whatever—will only be here for two weeks, so we need to use our time wisely. Remember I have to get back to my internship in Chicago. You understand, right? I would love to stay longer, but I just can't."

He blinked and his eyes fluttered for a moment.

"Of course I do. Two weeks should be enough."

❧

Like most old houses, every space was separated from the rest by a dividing wall, which meant there were doors everywhere, sometimes only leading to a hallway with another door at its end.

The main living and dining rooms were at the front of the house on either side of the main entrance. The kitchen, pantry, and keeping room were at the back of the house, facing south—toward the woodland and the valley below—and provided access to the outside deck. Beyond the kitchen, and adjacent to the garage, a short hallway led to Nick's study, a full bathroom, and a guest room, which I would be using during my stay. The rest of the bedrooms were all upstairs.

Nick and Mimi, as far as I could tell, had never paid much attention to trends in home decor. The stuff they had was simply what they'd acquired over time, what had been a part of their lives and deserved to be on display. Nick, for example, collected antiques and crafts from around the world. Many of them had fascinated me as a kid, and I would spend time admiring them and wondering about their origins and their meaning. They offered a glimpse into other times and other places, and perhaps an insight as well, the notion that the world of human beings stretching back in history was vast and strange and full of mystery.

On a lamp table beside the couch was a Greek statue, which I immediately recognized. It was a young man sitting on a rock. He wore a fancy-looking helmet that covered the sides of his face and had a huge decorative plume, like a grand crest. It made him look funny, and I thought the whole arrangement would be quite impractical in battle. Nick had spoken of him many times, but as much as I tried, I couldn't remember his name.

"What's the name of this guy?" I asked, looking at the statue.

"You *know* who that is," said Nick. "I told you his story a million times."

I felt a bit embarrassed, suddenly realizing I was able to remember trivial details like ice cream and pigtails but had forgotten almost everything about the heroes Nick loved so much.

"This, my dear Andy," he said, "is Theseus." He walked over to the statue and lifted it with both hands. "It's a replica of a monument that stands in Athens. Isn't it beautiful?" He looked at it for a while, smiling. Then he gave me a puzzled look. "You really don't remember him?"

"Now that we're talking about him, I remember he was a great king." I wasn't sure if I was remembering or guessing. Then I added, trying to explain myself, "my mind has been on other things, Nick. And besides, we haven't talked about the heroes since I was thirteen. You can't expect me to remember all that stuff."

He nodded as he studied the statue, feeling its weight.

"Yes, yes… I know, I know…"

"Why don't we take a walk?" I proposed. "I wouldn't mind stretching my legs."

"Yes." His eyes lit up. "The afternoon is beautiful, and there's a nice breeze. In fact, let's go out through the kitchen door so I can show you the backyard."

We stepped onto the deck, which was a plain wooden surface with a classic railing. It was modest, almost bare, but the views it offered were gorgeous. One could see the whole valley, all the way to the other side, where the woodland blurred with gray blue hills on the horizon.

"You see that mass of vines and thistles at the end of the yard? There"—Nick pointed downward to where the forest began—"see how the vegetation forms a crown with an empty center? That's the first flight of stone steps."

I nodded. Once I had that first reference, I quickly identified the other two sets of steps and then it was easy to figure out the whole layout with its four flat terraces descending all the way down to the woodland.

"Where's the firepit? If memory serves me, it should be on the second terrace," I said.

"Good! Right there"—he pointed to a cluster of thorny thistles with white flowers—"under the thistles, of course."

"What's that over there?" I pointed to a small square roof of black shingles toward the far right of the property. It seemed to be resting on a mass of ivy that emerged like tentacles from the ground.

"That's the shed. I can't even get to it anymore… which is a bit of a problem," he grunted. "That's where I keep the tractor and all my power tools." He waved his hand, changing the subject, and pointed to the far end of the slope. "At the very bottom of the property lies the forest you used to explore as a kid. Remember?"

I told him I did.

"Let's walk up the road then," he said, "and see what other things you can remember." He put his hand on my shoulder. "I can't believe how tall you are. You've grown more than the weeds back there."

༄

It was a short street, about three hundred yards, give or take. The front of Nick's property took up almost half the distance to the intersection and was marked off with a wooden fence. The grass and thistles grew thick and tall all the way and seemed to be pushing against the boards, trying to break through into the neighbor's lot.

On the other side of the fence, the shrubs had been trimmed to symmetrical perfection and the pines lining the property limit were evenly spaced.

"Snopengaard's lair," said Nick, pointing to the house with his chin.

It was similar in design to Nick and Mimi's house, with the same exact layout and materials, but everything about Snopengaard's home was obsessively manicured. The siding and trim had been recently painted, and the door knocker was polished bright. The roof looked as if it had been power washed the previous day, and the soffits under the eaves appeared to be brand-new.

"How long have the Snoops lived there?" I asked.

"Forever. They are part of Arcadia's landscape. He comes from a Danish or Swedish family; I can't remember which. Somewhere in Scandinavia. Karl Snopengaard. He calls himself 'Chuck.'" Nick shook his head. "I don't like him."

"Why don't you?"

Nick seemed surprised and gave my question some thought.

"I suppose he doesn't mean harm, at least not always. He's very earnest. It's funny just how seriously he takes everything he does, even nonsense. But he's also sleazy, you know, as if he was disguising his intentions. And his wife, Irina, is no better. She's a Russian lady, doesn't talk much. They never had kids."

We reached the corner where the street ended and connected to the main road, making an L shape. It stretched out as far as I could see and was flanked by the wood rail fence I had noticed on my way there.

"By the way," I said, remembering, "Mr. Higgins drove me here from the station. He says hello."

Nick nodded.

"He told me a friend of yours owns that house." I pointed to the mansion at the top of the hilly pasture. "Mr. Collins or something like that."

"That's the Collinsworth Estate," said Nick, looking up toward the house. "It's one of the many farmlands on which Arcadia was built. As a matter of fact, of all the original farms, it's the only one that was never subdivided for residential use. No one lives there anymore, but they have a property manager who keeps it all in good shape."

He looked around, using his hand as a shield against the afternoon sun.

"On the other side of that slope"—he pointed toward the south—"they keep a large orchard. It's really something. Apples and peaches and plums. And the house is majestic. A proper nineteenth-century château, in my opinion. Old money…"

"So, why is it empty?"

"Old Collinsworth, the original owner, refused to subdivide and sell, even during the 1960s, when Arcadia was at its highest point and the land was expensive. He died in the 1980s and passed the property on to his two sons, Archie and Greg. Archibald died in a car accident shortly after, and Gregory became the sole owner of the estate. He's about my age.

"When your father was a little boy, we and some other neighbors would go over to Greg's every now and then. The kids would play in the field, and the adults would drink highballs. It was great. Many years after, Mimi and I took you there once to eat cake and run around. You were quite small."

I vaguely remembered that.

"Then Greg moved to Manhattan and made a fortune with all that funny money in Wall Street. He once tried to explain what he did. He said he made and sold something like"—he grimaced as he tried to remember—"something like a 'bond sandwich.' Can you believe it? I think that's what he called them, 'bond sandwiches.' He said it was a way of putting a bunch of bonds together to even out the risk." He chuckled and shook his head. "But every time he said, 'bond sandwiches,' all I could think of was a food truck, with Greg wearing a white cap, slicing rolls…" He cracked up with laughter. "The world has gone a bit crazy, you know?"

"But you still haven't told me why it's empty."

"Ah, yes. Greg decided to keep the property after he moved out. Sentimental value, I suppose. Whenever he's in town, he comes to see me. We take nice walks around the property, and I sometimes return home with fresh apples or peaches from the orchard."

When we were back in the house, Nick excused himself and went up to his room for the night. He was tired, he said, and apologized once and then again, insisting I make myself at home and suggesting options for dinner, which I was to find in the fridge. I assured him I was alright and would do as he said, but as soon as he disappeared up the stairs, I stepped out onto the deck and found a comfortable chair. The sun was sinking below the tree line, and the valley turned orange and then began to flicker and dim.

I wasn't hungry. I just had a lot on my mind, and all I wanted was to sit there in silence.

If I was at Lindenfield, I would go for a walk, I thought. *That always does the trick.*

But as much as I tried to relax, my stubborn thoughts refused to quiet down.

Mimi's last breath.

Running up and down the stone steps.

Nick all alone in the dark house.

Your choices are yours, and yours alone, Andy.

Collinsworth and his bond sandwiches.

The LPS meeting and the long list of people I was supposed to shake hands with.

He should move closer to Bradwick, Andy.

Snopengaard trimming his bushes into neat squares.

Fancy talk like that is what makes the world an ugly place.

Theseus, the great king of Athens, and his funny helmet.

Ice cream and pigtails.

Sally and her pretty face.

I couldn't keep still and began to pace. It was almost dark, and I could barely see the yard below, but I didn't need any light to know what lurked there. Weeds and vines and grasses and thistles, braiding and spreading, conquering square footage and claiming it for themselves, like an insatiable green monster.

Are you sure this is where you're supposed to be?

CHAPTER 6

SLEEP CAME ONLY in the early hours of the morning, and it was troubled. I tossed and turned and dreamed all sorts of nonsense. I felt cold at times and hot at others, and no sleeping position seemed to work for more than a few minutes.

When I opened my eyes, it was past nine. Light seeped through gaps in the blinds, but it was barely enough to define my surroundings.

It must be overcast outside, I thought.

I stretched and sat up and felt calm and collected as if my restless night had somehow purged all the conflicting chatter and allowed me to see the world in practical terms.

I had returned to Arcadia for a reason: to help Nick get back on his feet. And what Nick needed was getting that yard under control. So that was exactly what I would do. I was also determined to get back to Chicago for my internship. I had promised my mother I would catch up with my reading and show up at the office sharp and ready to go.

I had two clear directives and exactly two weeks to accomplish them.

I most certainly am where I'm supposed to be, I told myself.

❧

When I walked into the kitchen, there was no sign of Nick. I started the coffee machine and called out, but no one answered. I went upstairs, but Nick wasn't in his room, nor was he anywhere else in the house. I called his phone, but he didn't answer.

I returned to the kitchen and only then realized there was a note on the counter.

> *Went into town to run some errands.*
>
> *Make yourself at home.*

I poured some coffee into the largest mug I could find and sat in the dining room, staring at the yard, still determined to accomplish my mission but not quite sure how to get started. Without Nick for guidance, I didn't really know what to do. I didn't know what tools to use, where to find them, or what to do with them.

By the time I poured my second cup, I had become impatient and decided to get started one way or another and figure things out as I went along. *Cutting down plants can't be that difficult*, I told myself. But then I remembered what Nick had said the day before: that his tractor and his power tools were in the shed—that small building to the right of the yard, completely surrounded by thick, braided vines.

After a moment's hesitation, I made up my mind to start anyway, even if I had to work with my bare hands. I would start with the vines on the side of the garage, which were the closest to the house. They had been the first thing

I saw when I arrived, so it somehow made sense to start with them.

The vines must have been no more than five yards from the walkway where I stood, and to reach them, I had to get across tall grass and thistles. I began wading through, but after just a few steps, the thistle thorns pierced my clothes and dug deep into my skin. I was forced to retreat.

I had faced my first defeat in only twenty seconds.

My next attempt was a bit more thoughtful. I used my shoes to bend the stems of the thistles at the lower end, where there were no thorns. Once the stalks pointed sideways, I stomped them until they were flat on the ground. With this technique, I succeeded in making a precarious path and eventually reached the wall.

I studied the vines for a moment. There seemed to be a variety of them—not just one species—and they wove into a mesh, forming intricate patterns, twisting into braids, and making their way up to the roof. My first impulse was to give them a good tug, but that only produced a shower of debris—mostly dead leaves—which fell on my head and got into my hair. The tug also scared the many living creatures that had made their home there and sent them scurrying in all directions. That gave me a hell of a fright, and the hair on my arms stood on end.

I tried again, this time with a better grip, feeling my way into its depths, scouting for thicker stems with my fingers. Once I had a firm grip, I yanked as hard as I could and managed to loosen a small section. I realized the outer layers, a few inches in, came away easily if I pulled them, because they weren't anchored to the wall but had latched on to other stems beneath them, one layer gripping onto the previous one.

The older, thicker layers—those that had stuck to the wall—were much more stubborn and consistently defied my grunting efforts as if they were a part of the house and inseparable from its structure.

☙

By midday, the wall was almost clear. Well, that might be a bit of a stretch. I had managed to tear off a significant amount of vegetation, which was piled beside me in a tall heap, but there were still a few stubborn layers that clung to the stone and mortar.

From the knee down, the vines remained practically untouched. Their stumps were thick—impossible to pull out—and were mixed with sharp blades of grass, so when I pulled them, they cut into my palms and scored my forearms, forming red lines across them.

The sky was overcast, and the air was hot and sticky. I was drenched in sweat and could feel the warm glare of the sun coming through the clouds and tickling the back of my neck. As I stood there, resting my hands on my hips, trying to make up my mind on whether the morning efforts had been a success or a complete waste of time, I felt a cool drop on my cheek. Then another.

It began to rain and then to pour and I had to dash for refuge under the front porch.

The tiny cuts on my hands and arms began to bleed, each producing a single droplet of blood, which mixed in with sweat and dirt and raindrops and trickled to the floor.

They stung as well.

Badly.

It dawned on me as I stood there—bloody and grimy—that the rainy season wasn't over yet. Storms would be frequent and would bring heavy rain for the rest of the month, interfering with our work in the yard. Suddenly, the whole endeavor felt impossible, insurmountable.

What the hell am I doing here?

It was still raining thick and heavy when I was done showering. I felt sore, and the back of my neck had turned a furious red. I called out for Nick again, but there was no answer, so I wandered around the empty house for a while.

Eventually, I found myself in Nick's study. It was a strange room. One of its sides had once been the exterior wall of the house and was made of fieldstone, roughly chiseled and joined with thick layers of mortar, like something you might see in an ancient castle. The study also had a vaulted ceiling, which made it feel bigger than it was and gave it a certain gravitas.

The opposite wall was covered with shelves, stretching from floor to ceiling and holding a considerable number of books, although some of them were reserved for antiques and other objects. A section of three shelves was dedicated to a collection of vases, all different sizes and shapes. I had seen similar ones before, and I knew they were Greek.

Amphorae, I remembered.

One of them was larger than the rest and stood out. It had a narrow base, becoming wider toward the top, with a pair of curved handles sprouting from the lower body and curving outward. It was glazed black and had scenes with figures and patterns in bright orange.

I scanned the books on the shelf. Homer, Ovid, Apollodorus, Apollonius, Euripides, Plutarch... I ran a finger along their backs and switched to the next shelf.

When I reached the end, I was about to move on, but a strange-looking book caught my attention. It was small and green and looked really old, perhaps because its spine had the typical embossed bindings of antique books. The title had been printed in gold letters, which were faded and barely visible. I pulled it back with my index finger and flipped through the pages. The title read *Heroikos* and was written by one Philostratus.

"That's an interesting read," said Nick out of nowhere, startling me.

I fumbled with the book and almost dropped it.

Nick looked younger. He had trimmed his beard and combed his hair. Even the skin on his face looked tighter and fuller. I was impressed, and I told him so.

"I have my days. Some good, some bad. You'll see. But most of the time I'm my usual strong and handsome self." He winked and I laughed. The Nick I remembered from all those years ago was alive and well and standing right in front of me.

"Where have you been all day?"

"I had to drive to Harrisburg. Boring stuff." He waved his hand, dismissing the subject. "The book you're holding is way more interesting than anything that might have happened in Harrisburg."

"What's it about?" I asked.

"Well, it's basically a dialogue, a conversation between a Phoenician merchant and a vinedresser."

"What's a vinedresser?" I asked.

"A vinedresser is like a gardener," said Nick, looking out the window, "or a groundskeeper. Someone who pulls weeds and vines and keeps a place neat and clear of unwanted vegetation."

He sighed and I looked outside as well at the green mesh of vines that sucked up the rain like a sponge.

"This particular vinedresser," continued Nick, "is taking care of a sacred garden, the tomb of a famous hero. As the merchant walks by, both men have a long conversation about Greek heroes."

"That's it? Just two guys talking?"

"What do you mean 'just two guys talking'?" He laughed and shook his head. "Philostratus was a very clever guy, you know? He wrote this dialogue to reimagine the heroes of Troy and think about their stories in a different light."

I shrugged. "It still sounds like two guys talking."

Nick smiled and thought for a moment.

"You're right, I suppose," he said softly. "But here's the thing, dialogues like these are very important; they help us think about stuff. A good conversation sheds light on what we don't know and also allows us to reconsider what we think we know; it provides perspective."

I ran a finger gently over the gold-leaf letters on its cover.

Heroikos.

"Remember when you used to tell me about the Greek heroes?" I asked after a while.

Nick nodded.

"What's the story with you and the Greeks? I mean, you've always been interested in them"—I looked around, signaling his library and the Greek vases as evidence—"but how did it start? What drew you to them in the first place?"

"I haven't really thought about that," he said and rubbed his beard. "It seems to me they've always been a part of my life. I taught the classics for decades, and as I'm sure you know, Greek mythology has been a great source of inspiration for Western literature so…" He trailed off and remained very still. "Although now that I think of it, someone told me the story of Theseus when I was a child. I think I heard it from a teacher at school. You know Theseus. We talked about his statue yesterday."

"Yes," I said, "the king with the funny helmet."

Nick nodded. "I was so captivated by his story, so… mesmerized. I suppose that's how I got hooked."

"Won't you tell it to me?"

"But I told you his story a thousand times when you were a kid."

"I only remember parts of it, and they're all mixed up in my head." I looked outside. "Besides, it's still pouring rain, so there's not much we can do for the yard right now."

"Okay then."

Nick sat in the leather chair that was tucked in one corner and I sat on the couch. A long pause followed, and all I could hear was the rain tapping on the roof. It was a constant drumming, like a ceremonial tambourine marking the beginning of some sacred ritual.

CHAPTER 7

"I THINK I'LL need some help from the Muses," said Nick, chuckling. He rubbed his hands and looked around the room. "It's been a while. Let's see… Let's see."

He closed his eyes and became very still. The rain tapping on the roof marked the passing of time, but it was hard to say how much of it had gone by or how quickly or slowly it was passing. Nick didn't seem to notice. He was in no hurry.

"Okay," he said finally. "Theseus was a prince, the son of Aegeus, ruler of the kingdom of Athens. As you know, he eventually became king, and a very famous one for that matter. There are many, many stories about him, but he's mostly remembered for killing the Minotaur. You remember the Minotaur, don't you?"

"Yes," I said, but I wasn't certain. "It was a monster, half bull and half man, right?"

"Right. The Minotaur lived on the island of Crete. It had the head of a bull and the body of a man. How that creature came to be is a rather complicated story, but what you need to know is that it was so ferocious and destructive that the king of Crete commissioned the construction of a huge labyrinth to keep it contained. This labyrinth was an intricate network of tunnels, branching out in mesmerizing patterns. It was full of twists and turns, false starts and dead ends. It was so intricate that anyone who entered would become disoriented and unable to find their way out. And while they went around in circles, the Minotaur would lurk in the hallways, sniffing the air, relishing the prospect of human flesh."

"That's horrible," I said.

"And it gets worse. There was a feeding ritual for the Minotaur."

"A feeding ritual?"

"Yes. Every year—though some versions of the story say every seven years and others, every nine years—Athens had to send seven young boys and seven young girls to Crete to be fed to the Minotaur."

"Why?" I asked.

Nick seemed to consider this for a moment.

"That's another long and rather complicated story, but the short version is that Crete and Athens were at war and Aegeus was the one to surrender. One of the terms of his capitulation was that Athens would provide these tributes, these young boys and girls, to appease the ferocious Minotaur."

"And you told me these stories when I was a kid?"

Nick chuckled. "You couldn't get enough of them."

"So, what happened?"

"Well, Theseus resolved to join the group of youngsters, travel all the way to Crete, and kill the monster to end this horror once and for all. King Aegeus tried to dissuade his son but realized there was nothing he could say to stop him. He did, however, ask Theseus for a special favor. If he was successful in his quest, he should change the black sail of the ship to a white one, as a sign that he was returning to Athens alive. Aegeus would look out for this sign every day, hoping to see his son return home safely.

"And so, the ship set sail for Crete, and the young tributes were brought before the king. Theseus stood tall among them, and his presence didn't go unnoticed, especially by the beautiful Princess Ariadne, who fell instantly in love with him.

"On the night before the feeding ritual, Ariadne sneaked into the prison and gave Theseus a sword and a ball of thread. She explained that by unwinding the thread, he would be able to navigate the labyrinth and eventually find his way back out. She made him promise that if he succeeded, he would take her back to Athens and make her his wife. Theseus agreed.

"The next day, Theseus tied one end of the thread to the entrance of the labyrinth and made his way into its depths, holding his breath at every turn, expecting to find the Minotaur lurking in the dark. The other tributes screamed in despair and wept as they sank to the floor and braced their knees, too afraid to turn the next corner.

"But Theseus pressed forward, taking one turn and then another, descending toward the heart of the labyrinth. Eventually, he came face-to-face with the terrible creature and killed it. Some versions of the story say he used his sword—the one Ariadne had provided—but there are other versions in which he used an iron club, and yet others in which he killed the beast with his bare hands.

"In any case, the triumphant Theseus followed the thread back to the exit and led the young Athenians to safety. In the dark of night, they scrambled to their ship and set sail back to Athens. And with them, as promised, they took Princess Ariadne.

"On the second day of their voyage, they stopped at the island of Naxos to fetch water and spend the night. But when they sailed off the next morning, Princess Ariadne was no longer among them. In some versions of the story, Ariadne was abandoned by an ungrateful Theseus, who decided to leave her behind once she was no longer needed. Apollodorus, however, gives a different account. In his version, the god Dionysus saw Ariadne sleeping on the beach and fell in love with her. He stole her away and made her his wife, leaving a heartbroken Theseus to sail home by himself.

"Theseus, according to this version, was so distraught that he completely forgot about the promise he had made to his father and left the sails unchanged.

"Back in Athens, King Aegeus climbed all the way up to the lookout on Cape Sounion, as he did every day, fixing his eyes on the horizon, hoping with all his heart to see white sails approaching. On that fateful morning, the king held his breath as a dot appeared on the distant horizon. But as the ship drew closer, its black sails were unmistakable, and Aegeus's heart sank into a pit of sorrow, possessed by an unspeakable grief. He stared down at the foot of the cliff, where the waves crashed against the rocks. It all looked blurry through his tears. Then he let himself fall…"

"He thought Theseus was dead," I whispered.

Nick nodded.

"Theseus inherited the throne from Aegeus and became a legendary king of Athens, uniting all the kingdoms of Attica. For centuries after, he would be worshipped far and wide as the embodiment of the perfect Athenian. As for King Aegeus, the sea to which he flung himself came to be known as the Aegean Sea and still goes by that name today."

We sat in silence for a while, and Nick stroked his beard. The room was dim, with nothing but the soft gray light coming in through the window. It shone on Nick from one side, casting deep shadows on his face, sharpening his features and making his eyes glimmer.

"Did these things actually happen?" I asked after a while. The question had been on my mind. "I mean, it's obvious that the Minotaur wasn't real. But the fact that the sea was named after the old king makes me think he might have been a real person."

Nick nodded as he considered this. "Some parts of the story might have actually happened. Others might have happened, but not exactly in the way the story tells them. And you're quite right, other parts might have been completely made up, a product of human imagination."

"So, Theseus might have been a real person who became the king of Athens?"

"He might have, yes," said Nick.

"But was he?"

Nick shrugged.

"I see." I was a bit disappointed. "And what about the labyrinth and the Minotaur?"

"Well, during the Bronze Age, the people of Crete—known to us as the Minoans—were the first advanced civilization of Europe, and they controlled all the important maritime routes in the region. But at some point in their history, this great civilization began to decline and they eventually disappeared."

"What happened to them?"

"We don't really know, but some historians believe their decline was caused by a series of invasions from mainland Greece, right about the time when Theseus was king of Athens."

"So, Theseus could have been one of the invaders."

"Maybe. Or maybe, after consolidating the kingdoms of Attica, Theseus used his power to enforce better trade conditions with the Minoans. Perhaps the tributes that Athens had to pay were too high and Theseus managed to negotiate better terms or disrupt tributary relations with Crete entirely."

He looked at me as if he was expecting a reaction.

"In the story," he explained when he realized I hadn't caught on, "the high tributes that Crete imposed on Athens might have been represented as the youngsters being sacrificed to the Minotaur."

"Oh," I said, "now I see it."

"Others believe that the Minoans practiced human sacrifice as part of their bull worship. The invading Greeks, according to this theory, were so horrified with these rituals that they represented the whole thing with the story of the Minotaur."

"So, we don't really know what happened," I said. "It may have been this way, or it may have been that way."

"Exactly! We don't—and can't—really know what happened," said Nick and made a question mark with his eyebrows.

"So, what do you make of it all then if it's just a story?"

"Just a story…" Nick shook his head. "Just a story… Stories, my dear Andy, are very important, more important than what you might think. In fact, stories play a crucial role in the way we understand ourselves and the world we live in. We make sense of our reality by weaving our experiences into stories, with a setting, characters, and a plot. And most times, we don't even realize we're doing this."

I nodded as I considered the idea.

"The inverse also applies," he continued. "When we experience a story, whether we are listening to one or reading one in a book or watching a movie, we tend to connect with the characters. We mentally step into their shoes and experience the world through their eyes. We even make moral choices by agreeing or disagreeing with their actions.

"While on the surface we are enjoying an entertaining adventure, at a deeper level we are revising our values, motivations, and goals; we are facing our fears and wondering about our potential."

"I never thought of that," I said.

"And I'll tell you more. The story we are discussing is not just any story; it's a hero myth, which makes it really special."

"How so?"

"Well, myths are sacred stories," he said, staring at me intently. "They've been passed down from one generation to the next, and they are very old—thousands of years old. And somehow, despite all that time, they continue to excite us and make us wonder."

"And that makes them special?"

"I believe so. You see, these old stories still make us wonder because they point to something important about the human experience, something our intuition tells us to pay attention to. And hero myths even more so…"

"I'm not sure I follow, Nick. Something important about being human? Like what?"

He remained silent for a while and shuffled in his chair as he looked out the window.

"At their core," he said at last, "hero myths are about growing up; they're about personal transformation and the realization of our full potential. They help us understand our place in the world and the type of life that's worth living, and ultimately they guide us to become the heroes in our own story."

"Be the hero in your own story…" I muttered. I could see myself running up the stone steps, making my utmost effort to be faster than Achilles. Nick had said something when I reached the top, something about the steps and about a hero. All this time, I'd been unable to recall exactly what he said, but now, those words…

"I remember you saying that to me when I was a kid," I said in response to Nick's quizzical look. "That I should be the hero in my own story."

"That sounds like something I would have said." He laughed.

"So, let me get this straight: you're saying that, deep down, the story of Theseus is all about growing up?"

"Growing up to become the hero in your own story, yes."

"By killing a Minotaur? I don't understand."

"Well, the deeper meaning of a myth is not always obvious. In fact, what these stories mean has been the question of the ages, which many thinkers have tried to answer in their own way. The Romantics, for example, believed that myths were a metaphor of sorts, something we're supposed to think about and connect with in order to better understand the world. The psychoanalysts, on their part, believed them to be an expression of our impulses, our fears and our inner conflicts. And I could go on… There are many ways of thinking about them."

"But what do you think?" I asked.

"Well"—he patted his beard—"I think… I believe that words are not always enough to describe what it means to be human, how it feels to be alive in one's own skin. And I believe that myths are a symbolic language—like a picture in our minds—that express subtle feelings and intuitions before we are able to put them into words."

"So, how does that play out in the story of Theseus?"

"Well, let's see. You can think of the labyrinth as a journey. A special kind of journey. One in which you can't really see where you're going and can therefore take a wrong turn. It's a bit like life, if you ask me. Every fork in the labyrinth is a decision, a choice. We take the left or we take the right. Are we making the right choice? We don't know for sure. Every choice puts us on a path, and that path in turn takes us to our next choice. But are we heading in the right direction? Do our choices take us where we're supposed to be?" Nick shrugged.

I shivered.

Are you sure this is where you're supposed to be? I heard Sally say.

"As we grow up into adults," Nick continued, "we become owners of our choices and, ironically, we also discover that we'll never have any certainty that we're making the right ones. Just like a labyrinth…"

I felt my body stiffen and my mind shift as if something had been unlocked inside me. I heard my mother's voice in my head. *You're a man now, and your choices are yours and yours alone.*

Nick was still talking.

"Let's add something to the mix, shall we? Why don't we throw in a Minotaur?"

I laughed and gasped at the same time. "The Minotaur," I said softly. "What does *that* mean?"

"Both the Labyrinth and the Minotaur are complex symbols, and they both can be thought of in many different ways. Some see the labyrinth as a journey inward, winding into our own depths, to the very core of our being, something like an exploration of the unconscious.

"The Minotaur, if we see it this way, could be a representation of our deeper self—the primal aspects of human nature—and defeating the Minotaur could be seen as a way of maturing, of becoming more in control of ourselves. The psychoanalysts call this process 'sublimation.'

"But if you think of the labyrinth as the journey through life, then the Minotaur might mean something else."

"Like what? Like all the bad stuff that might happen to us?"

"It might." Nick smiled. "That's a good way to think about it."

"But?"

"Well, I'm not sure, if I have to be honest. But I'll tell you this: sometimes the monsters we fear are not what we think they are. They may be scary, but not necessarily bad for us. In fact, they may even be a necessary part of our growth and development."

I nodded.

"But the most interesting thing about this myth, dear Andy, is the method Theseus used to navigate the labyrinth."

"Of course," I realized. "He had that string, right?"

"Exactly. The thread of Ariadne is what connects all the dots and helps us make sense of the twists and turns of life. All the choices we've made are joined, one way or another, into a thread of meaning, the narrative of our own personal story."

Be the hero in your own story, I thought.

"Remember what we discussed about stories and their importance," continued Nick. "Stories provide structure, context, and meaning to what we experience; they connect the events of our lives to a 'why' and provide a sense of direction, even when we don't know where the next turn in the labyrinth might take us."

I wasn't sure what to say.

Nick looked at me with a strange expression, a hint of a smile in his eyes.

Then he told me this: "Greek heroes—and all heroes, in fact—are inseparable from their stories. There is no story without a hero and no hero without a story. And this goes for you as well. Your path in life is your story, and you—and only you—are meant to be the hero in it."

CHAPTER 8

IT RAINED WITHOUT stopping, tapping gently on the roof at times and pounding on it at others, filling the house with a roaring white noise as gales rattled the windows and made the studs creak.

What the hell am I doing here? I kept asking myself. *I should be in Chicago.*

Nick wasn't feeling well the next day. I had been sipping my coffee when he appeared in the kitchen doorway. His skin was gray, and his eyes had sunk into their sockets. He looked shaky and held the doorknob to keep his balance.

"Are you alright?" I questioned.

"It was a hell of a party last night."

He said this in a phlegmy, crackling voice, and it took me a moment to realize he was joking. I didn't laugh, though. I was alarmed. He didn't look alright. I asked again, but he waved his hand and made his way into the kitchen, dragging his slippers in short steps, like a geisha.

"I smell coffee," he grumbled, "which is what one should smell upon awakening."

"Are you sure you're alright?" I asked again.

"Yes. Yes. I told you already. I have my days. Some good. Some bad. Today's not great." The mug shook in his hand. "I may need a few more hours of sleep, that's all."

He looked outside, and when he realized it was still raining, he shrugged and gave me a droopy look.

I wouldn't be of much use anyway, he seemed to say.

I had my own aches and pains. The work I had done the previous morning had taken its toll. I was sore all over, and my hands still hurt from pulling vines. My forearms were red and swollen and crisscrossed with tiny cuts, which had developed red auras around them.

"You were lucky," said Nick.

"Me? How so?"

"You were lucky the vines on that side of the house weren't poisonous." He was looking at my arms. "Carolina Creeper, English Ivy, and Wild Grape for the most part. But those cuts were not made by vines," he said, pointing to my arms with his chin. "Those are grass-blade cuts. They go right through your skin without you even noticing."

"Yard work is tougher than I expected," I said, sliding my forearms under the table.

Nick grunted. "By the time we're done with all this, you'll be carved out of wood."

I scoffed.

I spent the day on my laptop, going over the reading material for my internship. Mother had sent a long list of documents for me to study. Beside each title, she had added the word *mandatory* in brackets, which I thought was redundant and funny, in a way.

All the information I needed was available on the

Grimshaw database, to which I had access as an employee. I'd had an employee profile since I was fifteen, and I knew my way around the system, inside and out.

I was also familiar with most of the "mandatory" reading material, but I studied it anyway. I guess it made me feel useful. It also served as a distraction from the rain and the notion that precious time was going by without any progress in the yard, the notion that I had made a mistake in coming to Arcadia in the first place.

The first package I covered was an overview of financing options for large-scale real estate projects. I reviewed the mechanics of private equity real estate funds, real estate investment trusts—also known as REITs—and syndicated equity funds.

I know it sounds terribly boring, but it didn't feel that way to me. Repetitive and a bit of overkill, perhaps, but not boring. There was an underlying sense of purpose in knowing those things. They were the building blocks of a larger plan, a plan to succeed mother as head of Grimshaw.

Some day.

I thought about kings and their successors, those being groomed to take over the throne. I thought of Theseus, the great king of Athens, and his adventure in the labyrinth with all its twists and turns and forks along the way.

I thought of Sally and pictured the lines of her face, her well-defined jaw, and the shape of her neck as she moved her head when she talked. Her eyes would widen, and her slender shoulders would shrug and swing. Her hands would dance around making gestures as if they were speaking a language of their own.

I should call her.

❧

The rain stopped in the early hours of Monday, and by the time we had finished breakfast, the sun had dried any remnants of the storm. Nick was feeling better and was back to his usual self, chuckling at his own silly jokes and jumping from one topic to another. My sores and aches had also disappeared—at least for the most part—and the swelling in my arms had receded.

It was time to get started with the yard.

With the proper tools, I hoped.

"So, now we get the tractor and mow the grass, right?" I asked, rubbing my hands in anticipation.

"Not so fast, cowboy," said Nick. "We need to get to the shed first. That's where I keep the tractor and all my power tools."

"Right," I said. I remembered the little square roof toward the side of the yard, surrounded—almost swallowed—by thick vegetation. "So, I suppose we wade through the grass and pull the doors open?" I knew that was unlikely. I had only been able to make a few steps in the thicket before being forced back by the prickly thistles.

Nick was shaking his head.

"That won't be possible. And even if we managed to get there," he said, "the doors are covered with several inches of woody vines."

The air in my lungs escaped in a long sigh.

"Let's gear up," he said.

We sprayed repellent and sunscreen on our faces, necks, and arms and then covered up with sun hats, gardening sleeves, safety glasses, and gloves. When we were done, Nick motioned with his arm and led the way to the garage.

"We'll have to do this like in the olden days. Have you ever used a scythe?"

I shook my head.

"Here," he said, handing me an old farming tool with a long, curved blade. It looked very sharp. "It can slice your leg clean off, so pay attention." He was all business. "We'll try it out here on the driveway before we go into the grass."

The scythe had two grips, one near the top and one midway down. Nick held the tool using both arms, one flexed and the other extended. He planted himself on the driveway right out the garage door and turned to make sure I was paying attention.

"Now," he said, "stand up really straight, legs wider than shoulders, and bend your knees slightly. Shift your weight gently from side to side, from one leg to the other, but keep your back straight."

He looked funny, as if he was performing an old folk dance.

"Now rotate your trunk, twisting to one side and then back. Good. That's it. Now, grip the scythe and draw an arch with the blade. No, that's too high. The blade needs to be in contact with the ground as you swing it."

"Won't that dull the blade? As it scrapes the ground, I mean."

Nick shook his head. "The blade is curved upward. See? Push down with your right arm and hold firm as you rotate. Don't be afraid."

I tried again, feeling the vibration of the steel blade as it scraped the asphalt.

"Good. Now let's try with the grass. Let's mow a pathway to the shed, shall we?"

We stood side by side, about eight feet apart, our shoes almost at the edge of the grass. Nick nodded and began scything, and I tried my best to replicate his movements. I kept my back upright and rotated my torso, letting the blade slide on the ground, forming a wide semicircle.

It was extremely satisfying. The scythe made slicing and crunching sounds, cutting right through grass, bushes, brambles, and woody vine stumps, leaving in its wake a neat arch of green debris, like a deck of cards on a casino table.

"Each time you swing back to the starting position, take a small step forward," said Nick. "There you go. Good."

Our movements became rhythmic, and we were soon synchronized, slicing through the chaos in unison and leaving behind a flush, clean surface. When we reached the shed, we cleared a fair perimeter around it, revealing thick layers of vines growing up the walls and blocking the door with their tight braids.

Nick walked around the structure slowly, observing the varieties of plants, occasionally picking some leaves for a closer inspection. When he appeared around the other side of the shed, he stuck out his chin and nodded in satisfaction.

"No danger here," he confirmed.

"What do you mean?"

"Nothing poisonous. It will make our job easier. Wait here."

He returned from the garage a moment later, carrying a strange, curved tool. It looked like a scythe, only small enough to wield with one hand.

"In order to remove the vines from the shed walls, first

you'll need to cut the thick stems close to the ground." He handed me the curved tool. "This is called a serrated sickle. It's pretty straightforward. You grab a bunch of stems with one hand and then use the sickle to cut the clump. The only secret is that you're not supposed to hack with it; it's more of a pulling and rotating motion." He pulled his arm toward his waist and rotated his wrist, demonstrating the movement. "Once they're all nicely cut, you'll be able to pull the whole thing from the wall. It should all come off in one piece."

"What are *you* going to do?" I asked.

"I'm going to rest. That's what I'm going to do." He chuckled and walked over to the shade of a nearby white oak, where he sat and covered his face with his sun hat.

The serrated blade was sharp, and it cut clean through the vines, even the thick ones. I worked methodically at first, grabbing and cutting at the appropriate height and then pulling sections from the shed walls. They did *not* come down in one piece as Nick had predicted, and each scrap I managed to tear demanded a huge effort.

As the minutes went by, my rhythm picked up and I sawed with increasing urgency. I clenched my teeth and pulled the sickle furiously and tugged at the vines with violent jerks.

Stupid vines.

I caught a glimpse of Nick out of the corner of my safety glasses. His shoulders quivered as he laughed. Apparently, there was something very funny about the way I was working. I ignored him and kept going until I had hacked my way around the structure, revealing the walls of the shed and, to my surprise, a small window and a double door, wide enough to get the tractor through.

It was close to midday when I was done.

❧

Nick pulled the shed doors open, and I was hit with the smell of aged wood, engine oil, and thick, damp air that hadn't stirred in years. There were stacks of scrap wood piled on shelves on one of the side walls. The opposite side had hooks from which a variety of gardening tools hung, barely swinging as our steps swayed the wooden frame. Parked right in the middle was a green and yellow tractor mower covered in a thick layer of dust.

My heart sank. I don't know what I was expecting, but the tractor had somehow become a symbol of hope, an assurance that we would have a chance, that we might, just maybe, pull this one off. But that piece of junk was going nowhere.

"Isn't she a beauty?" said Nick, patting the hood. "I got her in the late nineties. You weren't even born." He chuckled and mounted the seat. He turned the ignition, and it clicked but there was no response. He tried again.

"I didn't think so." He shrugged. "But you never know."

"What now?" I asked. "What are we going to do?"

"Well. The battery is dead alright. But I have a spare in the garage."

He returned after a moment and replaced the battery. I held my breath as he tried the ignition again. There was an oscillating drone that quickly turned into a choked moan as if the machine were trying to clear its throat and get some air.

Nick seemed unfazed.

"The gas might be stale, and the fuel system is probably clogged up." He twisted his mouth from one side to the other as he thought. Then he proceeded to drain the old fuel from the tank, disconnect the spark plugs, and shut off the gas line. He placed a pan under the engine.

"This is the drain bolt of the carburetor's fuel bowl." He pointed vaguely at the engine. "We need to get the stale fuel out of there."

He loosened something beneath the engine and stuck his tongue out as he felt his way up. I heard a dripping sound as the liquid drained. Nick wiped the parts clean with a rag and stuck the cloth up the carburetor to wipe it from the inside. Then he inspected the filthy rag and smeared the black stuff with his finger.

"No sediments… That's good."

Nick tried the engine again, but nothing happened. He closed his eyes and scratched his head, and I sensed frustration in him for the first time. Then he detached the fuel line leading to the carburetor and turned the ignition once again.

Nothing.

"Well…" said Nick, clicking his tongue, "that's just too bad."

"What?" I asked.

"Everything seems to be in order. The testing sequence only left me with one option: the fuel pump. I was hoping to see some fuel spurt, but, as you see, there's nothing, which means the pump is toast. We need to get a new one."

"No problem," I said. "I'll drive us to the store."

"I'm afraid that's not possible," said Nick. "This is a really old model, and they don't keep these parts in stock. I'll have to order the pump and have it shipped."

CHAPTER 9

THERE WAS ANOTHER note on the kitchen counter the following morning:

> *Off to town again.*
>
> *Clear the first flight of stone steps if you can.*
>
> *Don't forget to gear up!*
>
> *And watch out for the wineberries!*

Into town again? I thought. *What's this man up to?*

I made some coffee and sat on the front porch while the sun was still low. I was in no rush to wrestle with weeds and vines, especially to clear the first flight of steps. The whole thing felt rather pointless. Progress without the tractor would be slow and onerous, and it was Tuesday already, which meant I only had about twelve more days before I had to go.

Nick had a different take. He insisted we keep momentum, even without the tractor. He argued that each task, each small thing we accomplished, would bring us closer to the end goal.

I sat there for a while, sipping my coffee and wondering what to do next. The air was fresh and smelled of grass and wet earth. I took a few deep breaths and looked around.

The front yard was bigger than I remembered. I hadn't appreciated its size when Nick and I took our walk the first day. The distance between the front porch and the street was short—maybe five yards—but to the east, on the side of the house that ran along the street and met the neighbor's property, the space was huge.

As I squinted into the sun, trying to estimate the distance to the fence, I saw two figures walking toward me, casting long shadows on the pavement as they approached. I was tempted to go back into the house and get out of sight, but just as I was considering this, the taller figure raised a hand and waved.

I waved hesitantly in response. With the sun right behind them, I couldn't see who they were or what they looked like.

"Hello, dear sir," said a man's voice. "Isn't it a splendid morning?" There was something off about the man's tone; it sounded unnatural and strained.

Too friendly, I thought.

The couple reached the end of the street and stood there, facing the porch. With the sun now coming from the side, I was finally able to see them better.

The man was tall and very thin. He had curly brown hair and a receding hairline that carved a path around a solitary patch, just above his forehead. It reminded me of the path Nick and I had cleared around the shed, and I had to bite my lip not to smile.

He wore thick rectangular glasses, a short-sleeved, checkered shirt, and pleated khakis. The woman was heavyset with short hair combed down against the back of her neck and puffed out in feathered layers toward the top. She had a stern look.

I realized they were the neighbors an instant before they introduced themselves. *The Snoops...*

"I'm Chuck. Chuck Snopengaard," said the man, "and this is my wife, Irina. We live next door." He pointed to the end of the street and had to shield his eyes from the sun. "We remember you—isn't it funny? —from when you were a little boy."

"I'm Andy." I took a few steps toward them and stretched out my hand. "It's nice to meet you again."

"I hear you came to help your grandfather," said Snopengaard. "Isn't that a noble thing to do? A noble thing. Noble indeed."

There was something unsettling about him.

"It's good that you'll be helping with the yard as well." He elbowed his wife. "After all, this grass won't cut itself." He laughed, and it was a strange laugh, like a donkey making snorts and heaves.

"Yes," I said, with a dry smile.

Then I remembered the fines Nick had received from the township. This strange character was the township manager, and according to Sally, he practically ran Arcadia. My chest tightened, and I straightened my back, sensing a judgment of sorts. It dawned on me that they were inspecting the property, gauging our progress with the yard.

"It'll get done," I said, trying to sound reassuring. "It will look perfect."

"I have no doubt about that." Snopengaard smiled.

"Not a trace of doubt. With a strong young man like your-self in the house, I'm sure it will look *absolutely* perfect." He nodded and then stretched his neck as if to see behind the house.

"We're also working on the back," I explained. "Once the tractor parts arrive, we'll get all this nice and mowed."

Snopengaard was still smiling at me over his glasses when Irina tugged his sleeve, pointing at something with her chin. She was looking at the wooden fence that sepa-rated both properties. Vines had crawled all over it and formed a dense mat, so thick and heavy it was pulling down the rotting posts.

Snopengaard clicked his tongue and shook his head.

"We'll fix that as well. You'll see. Everything will look like new," I hurried to say, and instantly regretted my oblig-ing enthusiasm.

"As I said, I have no doubt about it. You're young and strong. All this"—he looked around and waved his hand—"will be no problem for you. But your grandfather…" He took in a deep, dramatic breath and clicked his tongue again. "Maybe we should all think about him. You know? What's best for him, I mean. The house is surely too big for a man his age, now that Emily… now that Emily has left us." He paused and looked down for a moment. "Maybe he should move to a smaller house, something more practical. Don't you think so?"

He didn't wait for a response.

"The housing market in these parts is dismal, unfortu-nately. As much as we all love it, Arcadia has turned into a… How can I put this?"

"Ghost town," said Irina with a thick accent.

"Yes, I suppose," continued Snopengaard. "In any case,

finding a buyer for a house like this won't be easy. I'd be happy to look into it. When the time comes, of course. I may be able to find a buyer, someone decent who would pay a fair price...." He trailed off. Then he seemed to remember something. "By the way," he said, "I happened to speak to your father not long ago. We talked about all this, and he seems to agree with me."

"I don't care what my father thinks," I snapped. "Nick is fine. Thanks for the offer, but we don't need your help."

The Snoops raised their eyebrows and exchanged little looks of alarm.

"Well," said Snopengaard, clearing his throat, "it was so very nice to see you again after all these years. We only wanted to stop by and say hello. We'll leave you to it now. You surely have your hands full." He smiled, but only his upper lip curled, exposing his teeth.

"It was nice seeing you too." I turned and went back inside.

I was still shaking as I geared up.

Who does he think he is? The emperor of Arcadia or something? Are we supposed to bow down to him? Stupid Snoop.

All of a sudden, clearing the stone steps and getting on with the yard felt imperative. I sprayed sunscreen and mosquito repellent on my neck and face, slid on the safety glasses, and put a sun hat on my head. Then I snatched a scythe from its hook, slammed the garage door open, and got to work.

I swayed the blade back and forth, slicing away at the thicket, grunting with indignation. I cut through everything that stood in my way: grass, ivy, and whatever stumps I came across.

It took me a while to clear a path between the deck and the stone steps on the first terrace, which were flanked on both sides by a thick mesh of thorny bushes. I used a serrated sickle to deal with them, taking much care not to graze my arms against the sharp points. The tool cut through their fleshy stems with ease, and soon I had piled two heaps of debris on either side of the structure.

The steps themselves were completely covered with a strange type of vine I hadn't seen before. It was full of short, slender thorns that looked like hair, and the stems curved over themselves, forming loops like razor wire above a prison wall. I tried to use the sickle to cut them down, but the blade simply pushed away the bendy stems, leaving the plants unharmed. I would have to hold them firmly to make sure the blade scraped against their side and cut through.

Securing my gardening gloves, I grabbed the nearest one firmly.

It was instant agony, as if I had touched a live wire. The pain was so sharp that I froze in shock, my hand refusing to let go. Countless little darts had cut into my skin, slicing through my gloves as if they were gauze.

Watch out for the wineberries, I heard Nick's voice in my head.

I let out a scream and stamped my feet, slowly opening my hand and letting the thorns slide out.

"Stupid plant from hell!" I yelled at the coils and kicked the air. "Stupid yard. Stupid Snopengaard. Stupid Arcadia."

When the pain eased, I sat on a small section of grass I had cleared and wiped the sweat off my forehead. The sun was high, and a sultry vapor rose from the ground. It was thick and fuggy, and I craved some fresh air.

I thought about Snopengaard. I could see why Nick disliked him. And that wife of his was no better, frowning with disapproval and pointing out faults without saying a word. To top it off, Snopengaard had brought up my father, as if having him as an ally would further his cause, whatever it was.

But what made me even angrier was that they had thrown me off my game, making me apologetic and eager to please, stuttering and promising obedience. I had surrendered to their judgmental looks and reprimands.

◈

"How's it going, young man?"

Nick was standing a few yards behind me, looking around to inspect my work. He nodded in approval, and then his face grew serious.

"Those are wineberries." He pointed at the coils of razor wire. "Ugly bastards. Their thorns will cut into anything."

"No kidding," I scoffed and made a fist with my throbbing hand.

"You're going to need these to deal with them," he said.

He was carrying two strange contraptions. One was a cutting device with long handles and a short, rugged blade curved like a bear claw. The other was a long pole with what looked like a metal jaw and a pedal at one end.

"This is an anvil lopper," he said, holding out the first tool, "and yes, it can slice a finger clean off. And this"—he extended his other arm—"is a good old-fashioned weed puller."

He proceeded to cut one of the larger wineberries, making sure he left a short stump a couple of inches above the ground. Once the prickly stem had fallen over, he clipped it gently with the blades and tossed the entire coil to one side. Then he struck the ground around the stump with the weed puller and pressed it down, putting his foot on the pedal and leaning his weight into it. As the tool went deeper, the jaws clamped around the root system, and when he twisted the pole sideways, the whole thing came clean out of the ground.

"Just like that! You see?"

"I see," I muttered through my teeth.

"Well, now you're all set up"—Nick rubbed his hands—"I'm going to take a little nap. I'll see you later."

I grabbed the tools without saying a word and began cutting away, tossing the coils to one side and pulling the stumps out with the puller. It was easy work—once I knew what to do, of course—and soon the red, thorny vines were all piled beside me, forming a huge heap. In no more than half an hour, the area was completely clear.

A soft breeze was finally stirring the air. It felt like a reward of sorts, which I accepted, letting it dry my sweat and refresh my skin. With the stone steps clear, I sat down on the first one and closed my eyes, allowing the sunlight to paint orange kaleidoscopes on my eyelids.

I remembered climbing those same steps as a kid, running desperately up the slope, trying to be faster than Achilles. Nick had looked at his watch and concluded I was, indeed, faster.

"Be the hero in your own story," he had said.

Am I the hero in my story?

I was a student, majoring in business. I would work in my mother's firm. And, at the moment, I was pulling vines and weeds in a little town in Pennsylvania.

Yeah, I thought. *It doesn't feel very heroic, honestly.*

From where I sat, I looked down at the yard, trying to take stock of what I'd accomplished. It wasn't much. Most of the surface was still covered in a thick mesh of green chaos. On the terrace right below me—the second terrace—I noticed a clump of thistles standing out above the grass, right in the middle of the space. It was the old firepit I used to make s'mores in when I was a kid.

The thistles around it looked familiar. They were the same ones I had bent with my shoe on the first day, and I knew they were easy to cut down despite their aggressive appearance. Besides, I had the anvil lopper, which would make the task much easier.

Why not, then?

I took the scythe and made a new path, this time connecting the steps where I sat to the cluster of thistles. Then I grabbed the lopper and the weed puller and dispatched the thistles.

Before I knew it, the area was clear and ready for use. The firepit itself was just as I remembered: a large square made of stone pavers, neatly set and properly masoned. It reminded me of an altar of sorts, a place for ceremonial burnings.

CHAPTER 10

LATER THAT DAY, Nick and I reconvened on the deck. The sky was a deep blue, and the warm deck boards were beginning to cool off in the afternoon breeze. Nick stood by the railing, taking in the view of the valley and then scanning the slopes below. Our progress in the yard was almost imperceptible, a tiny scar on a furry beast. He sighed and grumbled, and then, all of a sudden, he stiffened.

"The firepit," he said. "You cleared it." He grabbed my shoulders and patted my back. "I can't believe it, dear Andy."

He stared at the firepit, lost in his thoughts, and I sat on one of the deck chairs. My body ached from all the pulling and shoving, but the simple act of sitting and relaxing my back and limbs came as a strange kind of pleasure, a reward for a good day's work.

"I've been thinking about what you told me," I said, still looking out the valley.

"I say lots of things," said Nick.

"I mean… the thing you said about being the hero in your own story."

"Oh… that," said Nick and, when I said nothing further, he continued. "So, what's on your mind?"

"I guess I still don't understand how one becomes a hero. And I'm not sure I feel like one, if you know what I mean."

"I sure do." He tapped his lips. "You're the protagonist in your own story; there's no way around that. The question, I guess, is what makes your story a heroic one."

"Exactly!"

Nick remained silent for a long time, looking out onto the valley as it changed colors under the afternoon sun.

"Do you remember the story of Perseus?" he asked, finally.

I looked at the sky, squinting in search of an answer.

"Never mind," he said. "I'll tell you a bit about him, just to refresh your memory."

"It seems like a good time for a story," I said. The breeze had picked up, and the trees swayed gently, making a shushing sound.

"Alright then," he said. "Let me see… Let me see… Perseus grew up in exile on an island called Seriphos. He lived with his mother Danae and his foster father Diktus, who was a fisherman. But Perseus didn't belong there. He was the true heir to the kingdom of Argos, and his father was none other than Zeus."

"You mean, *the* Zeus?"

Nick nodded and made wide eyes.

"The king of Seriphos was a cruel tyrant called Polydectes. He had set his eyes on Perseus's mother and wanted to force her into marriage. Day after day, he would harass her, and day after day, the young and strong Perseus would stand up to defend her.

"Polydectes realized he would have to get rid of Perseus if he was to have his way, so he came up with a plan. He announced his intention to marry a princess from a nearby kingdom and served a great banquet to celebrate the occasion. All the men in the city were invited, and all of them were expected to bring horses as a contribution to the dowry. But Perseus, who was a poor fisherman, was unable to meet the king's demands.

"He was deeply ashamed so, maybe to save face, he declared in front of all the guests that he would bring the king any gift he named, even the head of Medusa."

"Isn't Medusa the one with snakes for hair?" I asked.

"Yes. Medusa was one of the three Gorgon sisters. She was a terrifying creature with scales covering her body and hair made of writhing snakes. But the scariest thing about her —her real power—was that anyone who looked at her would turn into stone. Many champions had tried to defeat her, but they all failed. In fact, they had all become stone statues, decorating the entrance of the Gorgon lair."

"So, what happened?" I urged.

"Well, the king accepted the offer and bound Perseus to his promise, demanding he left the very next morning. Perseus had no idea where to search for Medusa, or how to accomplish his mission, but as soon as he left the city walls behind, the goddess Athena appeared and told him he should travel to the land of the Hesperides. There, she explained, he would obtain all the things he needed to complete his mission."

"What's a Hesperides?"

"The Hesperides were nymphs, goddesses of the evenings and golden sunsets." Nick gestured with his chin, pointing at the setting sun and the orange light that flooded the valley. "They gave Perseus a set of magical weapons: a special backpack called a *kibisis* to safely carry Medusa's head, a helmet that would make him invisible, sandals with wings for him to fly around, and a sword. He also got a special gift from Athena, the most crucial weapon for his mission. It was a bronze shield, so well polished that Perseus could see his face in it clearly, like a mirror.

"Once he had all he needed, Perseus put on his winged sandals and flew over the sea to North Africa, where Medusa lived in isolation with her Gorgon sisters: Stheno and Euryale.

"The creatures were sleeping in their cave when Perseus arrived, so he moved as quietly as he could, tiptoeing around in the dim light. When he was close enough to the slumbering sisters, he used his shield as a mirror to look around until the horrifying face of Medusa came into sight."

"But he didn't turn into stone. Or did he?" I asked.

"Well, because he was seeing her through the shield, the powers of Medusa had no effect on him, and he was able to keep moving, getting closer and closer. One of the Gorgons—he couldn't tell which—stirred in her sleep and made a muffled screech. Perseus froze and held his breath. When the Gorgons settled, he waited in place until the three of them were breathing heavily again.

"When he was in position, he lunged toward Medusa and swung his sword, making a clean cut around her neck. Medusa's head rolled on the floor, and her dead body slumped to the ground. Perseus stuffed the head in the *kibisis* and fled as fast as he could, using his winged sandals to fly out of the cave."

"And what happened next?" I asked.

"Well, it is said that Perseus flew about with his sandals over much of North Africa. He whistled through the air and zipped from one point to the next. As he flew, drops of Medusa's blood fell to the ground, and wherever one landed, a snake would emerge. This was why, people believed, the land of Libya was so full of snakes.

"He also flew east to the land of the Ethiopians, where he rescued the beautiful Princess Andromeda. As the story goes, Andromeda was being sacrificed to a terrible sea monster named Cetus. The monster slithered on the beach toward the sacrificial altar and was about to eat Andromeda when Perseus reached for his *kibisis* and pulled out the head of Medusa, holding it up until the creature turned into stone.

"Perseus married Andromeda and returned to Seriphos to settle his debt with the evil King Polydectes. But upon arriving, he learned that the king had persisted in his advances on Danae, forcing her and Diktus to take refuge at the other end of the island.

"He was furious. He marched to the palace, and when the king demanded his gift, Perseus pulled Medusa's head out of the backpack and turned him and all his court into stone.

"Perseus eventually returned all the special weapons to the Hesperides and gave the head of Medusa to the goddess Athena, who carried it forever on her breastplate or on her shield." Nick paused for a moment and our eyes met. "Whenever you see a sculpture of Athena, be sure to look out for Medusa's terrifying head."

"I will," I said, nodding.

We sat there for a while. The sun descended past the tree line and cast its orange glow on the far side of the valley.

"It's going to be a beautiful night," said Nick, looking around, "and since you've cleared the firepit, it might be nice to have a cookout. What do you say?"

"You mean like a picnic?" I asked.

His eyes widened. "Not at all! I mean a delicious meal cooked on the fire." He looked around again and nodded. "I have a feeling you'll enjoy it."

In the kitchen, Nick set aside a large cast-iron skillet and a cutting board. On the counter beside them, he placed a saltshaker, an olive oil dispenser, and a knife and fork with long handles.

"There's a wooden bench in the garage," he said. "Would you mind setting it beside the firepit? It's leaning against the back wall, where the paint cans are stored. Once it's in place, be so kind as to take these outside, will you?"

I did as he said and then placed two garden chairs by the pit. Nick joined me a moment later, carrying a large metal tripod about three feet tall, which he placed on the opposite side.

From my second trip to the kitchen, I brought out a tray with chicken leg quarters and a mixing bowl with a variety of chopped vegetables, a loaf of French bread, a jug of ice tea, and some plates, knives, and forks. It was a heavy load, and I wobbled it down the steps until it was safe at its destination. Nick, in turn, made his way to the shed and returned with a decent pile of firewood and a small cooking grate.

"There's nothing like a good meal cooked on an open fire," he said as he stacked the kindling and logs into a square. Soon, flames began to lick the logs and bathe us in soft light. I was impressed with his skill, and it dawned on me that he had performed this little ritual hundreds of times.

When the flames died down, Nick spread the embers into a red, glowing bed, stacked what remained of the burning wood on the side, and added two new logs to the pile, which lit up instantly and sent a new wave of warmth to my chest and my face.

He held his hand above the smoldering coals and mumbled sounds of approval.

"It's cooking time," he said.

He placed the chopped veggies into the skillet with some olive oil and then worked on the chicken quarters, coating them with butter and garlic. Once he was satisfied, he arranged the chicken pieces on the grate and put the iron skillet on the tripod, right under the burning logs. Finally, he took the bread, spread some butter and garlic on it, and placed it in the corner of the pit, just out of the fire's reach.

It took only a few moments for the food to start sizzling. Fat from the chicken slowly dripped on the embers, and thin lines of delicious-smelling smoke rose to the sky. I thought of the gods and instinctively looked up at the stars.

"So, what's the story of Perseus about?" I asked.

"Well, for starters, it's a very old myth. Exactly how old, we don't know. What we do know" —he looked up—"is that its characters have been immortalized in the stars. There's a constellation for Perseus, Andromeda, and Cetus, the sea monster. And there are also constellations for Andromeda's parents, Cepheus and Cassiopeia."

"And what about Medusa?"

"Medusa is part of the constellation of Perseus."

"Don't you think she should have her own constellation?" I asked.

"I couldn't agree more," said Nick. "She's a fascinating character." Nick rubbed his beard. "In fact, she's one of the most recognizable figures in all of Greek mythology."

Nick took a long stick from the pile and pushed fresh embers closer to the food, spreading them beneath the grate. As the stick made contact with the embers, it began to smoke and, eventually, glow. Once he was satisfied with the distribution of the heat, he buried the smoldering point into the soft ground, snuffing it out.

He stretched over the fire and turned the chicken legs over using the long fork. They were golden brown, dripping fat onto the embers and creating little flares as they made contact. He sprinkled coarse salt on them and then scattered what was left in his hand over the veggies, stirring them to check if they were soft.

"And what about Medusa's power to change people into stone?" I asked when I was sure I had his attention again. "What's the story with that?"

Nick grunted.

"Yes. That. Well, here's a theory. The ancient people of the Mediterranean used Gorgon symbols to scare off evil spirits. For example, they would place Gorgon masks on shields and on the front of homes for protection. Their function was, put simply, to be scary."

"Like some kind of boogeyman."

"Yes. The word *gorgo*, in fact, means 'terrifying.' The idea was that Gorgons were so frightening that anyone who glanced upon them would become paralyzed with fear or *petrified*, which literally means 'turned into stone.'"

"Oh… Now I see."

"Medusa, in that sense, embodies the things we're afraid of, the fear that stops us in our tracks, preventing us from moving forward."

"So, Perseus kills fear?" I questioned.

"Let's say Perseus didn't let fear hold him back. He didn't allow fear to *petrify* him," said Nick.

When the food was ready, Nick passed me a plate with chicken, veggies, and a slice of garlic bread. The chicken tasted like heaven: crispy, moist, and salty. And the warm garlic bread was to die for. I ate voraciously and moaned as I chewed.

Nick added another log to the ashes and it lit almost instantly, bathing us in light again. I stretched my hands closer to feel the warmth and looked at the sky, shimmering with countless stars. The air was colder and I rubbed my hands closer to the fire.

"What else?" I asked. "Is there more?"

"There's lots more," said Nick. He stretched back and faced the stars, resting the back of his head on his palms. "Let's see. Well, Perseus gets his magical weapons. Remember?"

"Of course," I said. "What does that mean?"

"The whole business with the weapons can mean a number of things. I believe they represent some sort of divine knowledge, as in something very important to know. You can also think of them as new skills or abilities."

"I see."

"But there is one weapon that stands out among the rest. A weapon handed to Perseus by Athena herself."

"The shield," I said.

"Exactly!" said Nick, and he gave me an inquisitive look.

I shrugged. "I'm not sure I understand."

"Well, the shield is not just any shield, is it? It's a mirror." Nick sighed and looked again at the sky, scanning the stars. "Isn't that fascinating?"

"I can't… I don't really see what it means," I admitted.

"A mirror represents introspection," he said softly. "It's a way of looking at ourselves, of looking within. When it comes to fear, dear Andy, the biggest secret is that the Gorgon lives inside each one of us. Our fears are all in our own heads."

He stood suddenly and disappeared into the darkness, returning a moment later with more firewood, which he placed over the smoldering ashes. After a few moments, they began to smoke and flicker, and we were once again lit up in a warm glow. I stretched my hands toward the fire and felt a wave of comfort return to my body.

"And what are you afraid of, Nick?"

He seemed taken aback by my question and raised his eyebrows. "No one's asked me that in forever," he said. "I guess I'm afraid of the same things we all are: getting hurt, being alone, something bad happening, making a mistake, death. Those things."

We remained in silence for a while, staring at the flames.

"But I believe deep down we're mostly afraid of change, of leaving behind what's known and familiar. Fear lives in our thoughts about an uncertain future, and perhaps that's why we stick with what we know and stay on the path we're on." He smiled. "You wanted to know what makes your story heroic?"

I nodded.

"Well, remember that hero stories are about growth,

and to grow means to change, to move forward. I think the story of Perseus gets right to what heroism is all about, not the absence of fear but a will to face it, to recognize it in our own minds. It's the will to keep moving forward and taking that new path, the one that seems so scary at first."

The flames made dancing shadows on his face, warping his features into a ritual mask. Then he broke into a wide grin and leaned toward me as if to tell me a secret.

"But the real kicker of this story," he said, "is that once Perseus obtained the head of Medusa and carried it around in his backpack, he was able to use it as a weapon against horrible monsters and evil tyrants. You see, young man, learning how to deal with your fears makes you formidable."

Nick's face was suddenly bathed in a bright white light, like a halo. I was shocked and blinked to make sure my eyes weren't deceiving me. He was positively shining, like some divine apparition. Then the light moved away from his face and flickered on my legs, and I realized it came from a flashlight, wiggling about in the dark as its owner made his way toward us through the tall grass.

"Is everyone alright? I smelled smoke and saw fire."

It was Snopengaard, making his way toward us.

"What on earth do you want, Karl?" demanded Nick, shielding his eyes from the light. "What's the emergency now?"

Snopengaard finally reached us, panting. He rested his hands on his knees and took a few deep breaths. The flashlight was still in his hand, pointing straight at Nick's face.

"Would you mind pointing that damn thing somewhere else, Karl?"

"Thank God… everyone… is okay…" said Snopengaard between breaths.

"Don't be silly, Karl. We're just having a cookout. What's gotten into you?"

Snopengaard had finally composed himself and was standing there, pointing his flashlight at our faces, alternating from one to the other, oblivious to our forearms covering our eyes every time the beam was in our faces.

"Would you stop playing around with that damn light, Karl? Stop it!" said Nick.

"I must remind you, Nicholas," said Snopengaard in a formal, dignified tone, "that there are ordinances and regulations for backyard fires."

He finally turned the stupid flashlight off, and we were left in the dim light of the embers. It took my eyes a moment to adjust. Snopengaard was standing beside me, looming over me, still wielding a pointing finger after pronouncing his dictum.

"Don't you have anything better to do, Karl?" sighed Nick. "Aren't there any other neighbors around for you to harass?

"You should know better, Nicholas," Snopengaard retorted. "Regulations and ordinances exist for a reason. They ensure order and safety. They foster reciprocity and respect in our community and protect our property and our rights. Rules are meant to be followed"—he shook his head sanctimoniously—"but it seems you think yourself above them."

"Don't give me that nonsense, Karl. You really want to educate me on rules? I respect and follow rules alright. The real ones, that is, not the ones you make up as you go."

"That's outrageous, Nicholas!" Snopengaard didn't know what to do with his hands and looked around as if he was searching for something. He was flustered. "How can you say something like that? It's clear that you haven't changed. Not a single bit," he said between his teeth.

Then he looked at me.

"It's unfortunate you're exposing your own grandson to this irresponsible behavior. He seems like a bright young man. Let's hope you don't teach him the wrong lessons. You're always putting funny ideas into people's heads."

Nick's eyes fluttered in a moment of hesitation as if Snopengaard's words had struck a chord. It was hard to tell in the dim orange glow, but I could swear I saw Nick's face lose all expression. He remained silent, staring at Snopengaard.

"All I'm saying—" he stuttered, but Nick cut him off.

"Get off my property, Karl." He said it softly, without a hint of emotion, his eyes set on his neighbor and his hands folded over his lap.

Snopengaard looked around nervously and grimaced, unsure of what to do next.

"Very well," he finally said in a puffed-up tone. "My intention was only to serve, but seeing that my efforts are unappreciated, I will take my leave. But you'll hear from my office." His finger pointed vaguely in our direction. "This will be looked into… for the safety of us all… and this pit doesn't seem to comply with the minimum distance from nearby structures." He pointed nervously at the house and then at the firepit. "It's also late at night, so you are in violation of time restrictions. And besides"—he seemed to remember all of a sudden—"smoke is considered a 'disturbing nuisance' in our community ordinance."

"Good night, Karl," said Nick. He hadn't moved an inch.

Snopengaard turned on his flashlight again and began

making his way back. After crossing the strip I had mowed with the scythe, he came up against the wall of tall vegetation and was forced to wade across it, steering wide of the thistles as they appeared in the beam of light.

"Karl!" yelled Nick. "I saw a snake earlier today. And a pretty big one too. It was right about where you're standing. Watch your step."

Snopengaard let out a squeal, and the flashlight bobbed up and down as he hurried back to safety, lighting up random trees as it swung from one side to the other. Nick chuckled and I laughed. Then our laughs got louder, bouncing off each other, making the incident funnier and funnier with every heave. Soon we were both bent over, slapping our thighs and roaring in horselaugh.

CHAPTER 11

IT RAINED THE next day. At times, it was a heavy downpour and thick clouds darkened the sky, making the trees and terraces and vines look gloomy and sinister. Then it would ease into a monotonous pattering, raining just enough to force us indoors and prevent any progress in the yard. It was Wednesday, and it seemed to me that days were flying by.

Nick was sick again. He looked frail and emaciated, just as he had a few days before. He walked in his little geisha steps, dragging his slippers across the kitchen floor, mumbling something about coffee.

I told him he should see a doctor, but he dismissed the idea.

"Seriously, I'm fine." He shrugged and poured himself a cup. "Some mornings I just look my age. There's nothing I can do about that."

With nothing better to do, I spent the day on my laptop, going through Grimshaw documents from the database. I started with procedural and compliance modules, covering financial regulations, zoning permits, environmental standards, and building codes.

One by one, I crossed out the items on Mother's list of "mandatory readings." Just like my last session, the exercise felt a bit redundant. I knew most of the content well enough, and the few things I was not familiar with were pretty straightforward once I read them.

The last portion of the reading list was centered on Grimshaw's business plan, detailing income streams and outlining its projects in urban infrastructure and commercial real estate. There was a forward-looking section, which I read with interest. It showed areas of expansion and business development and promised a bright future for the industry and substantial returns for Grimshaw investors. I wondered if I would be in charge of one of those projects as it matured.

By midafternoon, I had crossed every line off the list and there were no more folders to open on the database landing page.

I guess that's it, I thought and pushed my computer aside. *All done.*

The movement must have made the mouse scroll down because at the bottom left of the screen a new folder came into view. It was titled *Others* and contained a large number of subfolders, more than any of the sections I had already gone through. Most of the documents inside each subfolder seemed to be works in progress, draft versions of material in development.

One of them was titled *Location Checklist and Criteria for Location Attractiveness.* It established a process to determine whether a town or locality held any promising return on investment, everything from proximity to larger cities, transportation networks, land availability, soil stability, and elevation. It went on to analyze infrastructure, business

environment, workforce, environmental and zoning regulations, taxation, administrative burden.… The list went
on and on. Each criteria had a grading system and a set
of instructions to determine the factors that would add or
subtract points.

It was still raining, so I figured I would do an
impromptu analysis of Arcadia, using this checklist and
criteria to the best of my knowledge. I followed the instructions carefully and weighed each data point, checking the
Grimshaw database for reference when I had doubts.

The results were horrible. Arcadia was dead, which was
no surprise. It was, after all, a rusty old town, its days of
glory buried in the past. It did feel unfair, though. Arcadia
had succumbed to changing times, tectonic shifts in the
global economy, and demographic ripples in the region.
None of those things had been its fault.

I decided to run the exercise again but made some
changes to the grading methodology. It was lacking some
important considerations, so I decided to further classify
the criteria and lay out the data on a grid, separating variables that were given and immovable—like geography and
topography—from those that could be improved through
investment, planning, policy, and infrastructure. Once all
the data was plotted and weighted, the conclusion was a
very different one. Arcadia had, in fact, huge potential. It
just needed a lot of work.

I texted my mother to report my progress. I thought
she'd be pleased. After all, I had completed my assignments
in less than half the allotted time.

"What are you still doing there?" was her first response.
"Finish up and get back to Chicago. You've already wasted
enough time."

I was considering what to reply when another text came in.

"I'll be in California until the end of the week. Here's another list of things you should read. They'll be part of the drill to prep you for the LPS."

A long list of articles followed.

My breathing became shallow, and my chest and arms tensed up. I began typing my plea for more time, begging for her understanding. I erased the words and began again. And then again. Three times. Five times. Every response I rehearsed played out in my mind with some catastrophic outcome. I couldn't make up my mind what to do. I was spiraling.

Then I realized my arguments would only escalate the situation, giving her something else to nibble at, another angle for her jabs. The best course of action would be some vague commitment, a little release from the pressure valve.

"I'm doing my best, Mom. I'll be there as soon as I can" was the message I finally sent.

I woke up thinking about Sally. I imagined her striding gracefully through the parking lot, her sharp shoulders swaying with each step. She had spoken to the bus driver, and they had both laughed. I liked her laugh. It was relaxed, and there was something true in it.

I texted her and we agreed to meet at the township building when she finished work. Nick was happy to lend me his car, so I drove along Redwood Road, winding my way through Laurel Hill and then straight to the main square.

The township building lobby had polished stone

floors and high ceilings. Natural light came in at an angle from tall, arched windows. The centerpiece was a massive staircase, which wrapped around the walls and led to the mezzanine on the floor above.

At the foot of the stairs was a sign that read *Main Office* and had an arrow pointing upward, which I followed until I reached the upper floor. It was a simple layout with an open space with desks on the other side of a long wooden counter. A handful of employees were at their workstations, and I caught a glimpse of Sally as she walked to her desk. She was wearing a long flowery skirt and heeled sandals, which made her look even taller than I remembered.

She saw me too and came toward me.

"Hello you," she said with a smile. "You're right on time. Let me get some things sorted and I'll be right back."

I leaned against the counter and looked around as I waited. While the building itself was ornate and imposing, the workspace was simple and efficient with a few desks arranged in a rectangle and two long, very heavy-looking rows of filing cabinets, one against the far wall and the other one running at a right angle on the street side. The only enclosed space was an office in the far corner. As I was looking at it, the door opened and out came Snopengaard, who saw me and walked toward me before I could react.

"It's so nice of you to visit, young Mr. Romano," he said in his high-pitched voice. "Are you here to pay your grandfather's fines?"

"No," I said. "I'm here to meet Sally."

Snopegaard looked surprised at first and then a bit disappointed.

"You know," he said as he adjusted his glasses, which had slid down his nose, "I feel you and I started off on the wrong foot. I hope you understand that I care about this town and about Nicholas and his well-being."

"I understand," I said without taking my eyes off him. Something in his demeanor made me uncomfortable. He fidgeted and his beady eyes darted around as he spoke. I could see why Nick didn't like him; he seemed to be up to something all the time.

"You got upset last time I mentioned this," he continued, giving me a condescending look, "but I feel compelled to bring it up again… for the sake of your grandfather, of course. I am pretty sure I could get a buyer for Nicholas's house. At a price that at least wouldn't be… How can I put this? A price that wouldn't feel like an insult, which in these parts, I must remind you, is quite something. Think about it. I hope you come to realize that it's the right thing to do. That yard is just too big for him to manage. And he's not getting any younger, if you know what I mean."

"How kind of you, Mr. Snopengaard," I said, forcing a smile. "I'll give it some thought."

"Well…" He forced his strange smile in turn. "I hope to see you again soon so we can discuss this further." He began to walk away and suddenly stopped and turned around. "And please remember your grandfather's fines. They won't pay themselves, you know?" he said and snorted his donkey laugh.

By the time Sally and I walked out of the building, the rain had stopped and we were able to stroll across the park, avoiding large puddles here and there.

"So, you study in Harrisburg?" I asked.

Sally wiped a bench with her hand and sat.

"Come on. Sit," she said with a playful smile.

I wiped the spot beside her and sat. Our arms grazed.

"I take classes at HACC," she said.

I nodded, but she realized I was clueless.

"Harrisburg Area Community College. I'll major in public administration."

"What's that like? What does a public administrator do?" I asked.

"It's mostly management of government programs. I study government organizations, how they work, and how they can better serve the public."

"I see," I said, and then I made the connection. "That's why you work in the township office during the summers."

"That's right." She gave me a funny look. "Maybe you're not such a dummy after all."

I laughed and she did too.

"Anyway," she continued, "during the school year I live in Harrisburg; me and two other girls rent an apartment downtown. I work a few hours a week for the Department of Public Welfare. It's just a clerk job, and the pay is not great, but I learn a lot. I love what I do."

"And the work here?" I signaled the township building with my thumb.

"It's alright, I guess. Arcadia is a small town, and there's not a lot going on. But the good thing about it is that I've pretty much learned how everything works around here. It allows me to see how a township is run from beginning to end. Like public administration in a petri dish."

"Is Snopengaard a pain in the ass?" I asked.

"Chuck? He's okay, I guess. He's polite and seems to care about the town. He's a stickler about rules and keeps mostly to himself. He's closed up in that office of his most of the time."

"What's his story?" I asked.

"He's been part of this town forever. My dad told me he and his brother grew up here. His brother—I think his name was Jon or something like that—died in an accident in one of the old factories, Bethlehem Steel. That was many years ago. Karl has been the township manager for as long as I can remember. I don't think he has any friends, except for 'The Three Elders,' and I am not sure I would call that a friendship."

"The Three Elders?" I questioned.

"The township manager is appointed by a board of three supervisors. I call them 'The Three Elders.'"

"And those are what, imperial overlords?"

She laughed. "No, numskull. Arcadia is what's called a second-class town, which means we are governed by a board of supervisors. Three supervisors. The board is elected every six years, and it's always the three old familiar names that get voted over and over."

"The Three Elders," I muttered.

"Exactly. They are the ones who appoint the township manager and have been Chuck's buddies since forever. They are basically the founding and only members of the Arcadian Brotherhood and the Historical Preservation Society and all those fun groups."

We both laughed again. Her shoulders quivered, and she tucked her hair behind her ear and straightened her skirt. Then she grew pensive.

"So, what's your story?" she asked.

"What's my story?"

"Yes. Your story, dummy. Aren't you going to be some sort of real estate mogul at Grimshaw?"

Theseus crossed my mind, navigating the labyrinth. *I was lucky in that sense*, I thought. *My path was clear enough.*

"That pretty much sums it up," I said, shrugging. "In fact, I should be in Chicago right now. I was supposed to start my internship at Grimshaw this week, part of my training to become a manager. The idea is that someday I'll take over from my mother. That's the plan, at least. And after that, world domination."

She laughed.

"So, what are you doing here?"

Our eyes met, and we both lingered for a moment.

"I'm… I'm not really sure," I said almost in a whisper.

"Come. Let's walk a bit," she said.

We strolled around the park, and she told me about growing up in Arcadia. She said it was sad to see so many people leave town. She would leave some day as well. Taking over Bernie's Ice Cream wasn't in her plans, and it didn't seem to be in the plans of her two younger brothers either.

"The saddest part is that nobody seems to want things to change. They seem quite happy with the status quo. For example, there's a planning commission for local initiatives and budget allocation. The meetings are open to the general public, and the agenda is listed on the website, but nobody ever attends. It's just Chuck and The Elders, keeping everything exactly the same as it's always been. And, between us, I'm not even sure The Elders are very involved. As long as Chuck runs things smoothly and there are no surprises, The Elders seem happy to give him full control."

That reminded me of the assessment I had done, and

I told her about it. I did it casually, as part of the topic we were discussing, but she was very serious and asked a bunch of questions about how it worked and what considerations I had used. She was taking mental notes of what I said, and she even asked me to send her a copy of the report.

"Sure," I said.

Then she took my hand and led me across the street to her father's ice cream shop. It was exactly the way I remembered it: an old-fashioned building with ornate moldings and accents and terrazzo floors.

"It's been this way since my grandfather opened it in the '70s," Sally explained. "It used to be a barbershop before that, in the good old times. My dad will tell you they don't make buildings like this anymore."

We sat on a bench on the sidewalk just outside the store and had our ice cream. It was so delicious, it made all the ones I'd tried before seem like failed attempts. The taste was sweet, but the flavors were vibrant and crisp, cutting easily through the sugar.

"It's got no heavy cream in it," said Sally, reading my mind. "Just egg yolk and sugar custard. That's what makes it so special. But don't tell a soul." She elbowed me and laughed.

The sky opened up, and the afternoon sun shone through, casting long shadows on the main road. A couple of stores were turning on their lights, but most were locking up and closing for the day. The lights at Bernie's went out, and the employees left. They waved at Sally as they passed us.

"Hey, Sal!" one said.

"Bye, Sally," said another.

A moment later, Mr. Higgins came out to greet us. He seemed happy to see me.

"Tell me about your grandfather. I was a bit worried, if I have to be honest, when we dropped you off the other day. Is he alright?"

I explained he had his days, but overall he was well. I told him we were working on the yard, trying to get everything looking good again.

"It's a mighty good thing you're doing there, son. Good for you," he said.

"I wish I could stay longer," I said. "These days I've spent in Arcadia have been great. It brings back so many memories. This town is very special to me."

Sally jumped in and told Higgins about my assessment.

"He has really good ideas," she said. "It turns out that with the right planning and policy changes, tax breaks, and some infrastructure, Arcadia could become attractive for businesses and new residents. You know, Andy is learning all this stuff from Grimshaw. I bet he could be a great asset for the town." She elbowed me and smiled.

"It was just a quick exercise," I protested. "It's by no means a thorough piece of work."

But Higgins insisted, asking me for the highlights, so I briefly explained the criteria and the parameters I had considered. He listened attentively and nodded occasionally. I told him about the overall score, which was bad, but then I explained how the low-scoring parameters were all fixable. With the right plan and sufficient capital, Arcadia could revert its trajectory. The types of industry and services the town would thrive on would be different from the ones that made it successful in the past, but in time, Arcadia could recover some of its former glory.

"This town needs young people like you, Andy. You've got a good head for these things. You should stick around during the summer, so we can talk some more, maybe meet up with Mr. Snopengaard and the board."

I shook my head. "As I said, I have plans for the summer. I need to get back to Chicago for my internship. Maybe some other time."

"That's too bad," said Higgins. "That's too bad."

CHAPTER 12

IT RAINED THE following day, and I began to lose hope again. *At this rate*, I told myself, *the yard work will never get done.* The bad weather dragged on well into the following day and only showed some signs of improvement in the afternoon. The pattering finally ceased and gave way to an annoying drizzle, and then even the drizzle stopped and the sky opened up.

Nick was feeling like his old self again, and he invited me to join him on the deck. He explained that a spring afternoon following heavy rain was a blessing; the air would be fresh and clear, and the sprouting valley would be looking its best.

He was right. I couldn't remember seeing the valley so bright and in so much detail. The sprouting trees painted the terrain green, with splashes of white and yellow where the brambles had bloomed. Rain droplets, still clinging to leaves and branches, reflected the afternoon sun, creating the illusion of a starry sky laying on the ground.

"You have one heck of a view," I told him. We were both resting on the railing, our eyes on the horizon.

"I love this place," he said, still looking out.

We sat on the deck chairs to chat and enjoy the breeze. I told him about my progress with the Grimshaw reading and how my mother never seemed satisfied. I told him about my visit to the township building and about Sally. I liked her, I said, and he chuckled and nodded. I told him I was worried about our work in the yard, and how the rain had set us back, but he waved his hand and told me not to worry.

We made some sandwiches for dinner and brought them out to the deck. The stars were out by then, impossible to count. They glowed as if they had to make up for lost time after being covered for two nights in a row.

"So, what hero comes next?" I asked when we had finished.

He shrugged. "What's been on your mind lately? What do *you* think comes next?"

"I don't know… I suppose… How can I know if I'm the hero in my own story?"

Nick thought for a while, and then he spoke slowly, as if he was thinking the words as he said them.

"Hero stories follow a pattern. They're roughly split into three stages or acts: Departure, Initiation, and Return. Once you become familiar with these stages, you can look at your own story and make more sense of it, maybe even figure out whether or not you're the hero in your own story."

"Let's talk about that, then."

"The first stage is the departure, in which the hero sets out on a quest." Nick pressed his lips as he thought. "You see those three stars in a line?" he asked after a while, pointing just over the southwest horizon. I could easily make out a line with three evenly spaced stars.

"That's Orion's Belt. He was a hunter. If you follow the line"—he dragged his finger sideways toward the south—"you can see the brightest star in the sky. It's called Sirius, or Canis Major, which the Greeks called 'The Dog.' There are actually two dog constellations, one next to the other." His finger made a vague circle around the bright star and the one right next to it. "Those are Orion's hunting dogs."

He pointed back at the bright star and then moved his finger further south, making an up-and-down motion, signaling a space below the horizon. "There used to be a very large constellation south of the dogs. We can't really see it from here, but it used to cover a big portion of the southern sky. It was really big."

"Why do you say 'was'?"

"Because it changed. Well, the map of it changed. It was called Argo Navis, and it was so big and covered so much of the sky that it didn't really work as a reference point. So, purely for practical reasons, astronomers decided to break it up into three smaller constellations. One of them can barely be seen from here." He pointed again, but I could only see trees. "There between those branches. That's the corner of the constellation Puppis, the Stern."

"So, what was this Argo Navis?" I asked.

"It was a ship," said Nick. "The finest ship that had ever been built. It took Jason and the Argonauts to the end of the world in search of the Golden Fleece."

I looked again between the branches, but there were no stars to see.

"So," said Nick, "I'll tell you the story of Jason, but just as the astronomers broke up the Argo Navis, I will also break up his story and tell you a part of it."

"Let's hear it."

"Alright then. There was a city in ancient Thessaly called Iolkos, whose rightful king, Aeson, was attacked and deposed by his half-brother, Pelias. Aeson's wife had just given birth to a baby named Jason, whom she smuggled out of Iolkos and sent away in secret.

"The evil King Pelias was eager to consolidate his power and gain dominion over all of Thessaly, so he sent his men to consult the oracle about his plans, but all they reported back was a simple warning: 'Beware of a man wearing one sandal.'

"The years went by, and when Jason was about your age, during the rainy season of his twentieth year, he made up his mind to claim his birthright, the throne of Iolkos. He wanted to be king, and he knew he was the rightful heir.

"So, he set out on foot, following the banks of the river Anauros, and made his way into the valley toward the city. As he traveled, the goddess Hera watched closely from Olympus. She wanted to know if Jason had the mettle to be the hero in his own story, so she resolved to test his character. She disguised herself as an old woman and waited at the bank of the river at the point where it became narrower, knowing Jason would likely pick that spot to cross.

"When Jason arrived, she asked him to help her get to the other side. Jason inspected the river and considered the matter. It was the rainy season, as I said, so the current was strong and the riverbed was full of treacherous boulders. But Jason nevertheless decided to help the old woman.

"Hera climbed onto Jason's back, and he began the difficult crossing, feeling the slippery stones before each step and leaning against the current to keep his balance. Slowly, step by step, he made progress and managed to get across the deepest section of the river.

"But just as he was reaching the opposite bank, one of his sandals got caught between two boulders. With the water rushing against him, he pulled and tugged to dislodge his foot, tearing the sandal and losing it to the current.

"Once on the other side, he continued his journey as best he could, limping along with his bare foot, and went straight to the marketplace when he arrived in Iolkos. The king was alerted about the stranger, and when he arrived at the scene, he was astonished and terrified to see before him the man of the prophecy, the man wearing one sandal.

"Jason cleared his throat. 'I have come to my home to recover the ancient honor of my father, for I am Jason and I am the true heir to the throne of Iolkos.' Everyone gasped. King Pelias was stunned and remained silent. After a long pause—and to the surprise of many—he told Jason he was willing to cede the throne on one condition."

"What condition?"

"On the condition that Jason bring him the Golden Fleece."

"What's that?"

"The Golden Fleece was a sheepskin, but not just *any* sheepskin. It was the pelt of the mythical ram of the constellation Aries." Nick turned around and looked at the sky behind him. "We can't really see Aries from here. It's right next to the constellation Andromeda. Anyway, the Golden Fleece was kept under heavy guard in the city of Colchis at the far end of the Black Sea, which was the end of the known world at the time."

"But why was it important? Why did the king want it?"

"There are many theories about what the fleece means, but most agree it was a sacred object, which had the power to make royal authority legitimate. And that, dear Andy, is what every king really needs: legitimacy. True and real power, not just a title."

I nodded.

"But King Pelias had selfish reasons to send Jason in search of the Golden Fleece."

"He was basically sending him away," I said.

"Exactly. A voyage to the end of the world was nothing short of a suicide mission, and Pelias knew it. Everyone knew it. He was sending Jason to his death but pretended to help him by commissioning the construction of a fine ship, which came to be known as the *Argo*."

I looked again toward the south, trying to imagine a ship made of stars, as big as the sky itself. Nick was still talking.

"Fifty great heroes from all the Greek kingdoms signed up to join the expedition and arrived in Iolkos to board the *Argo*. Those champions came to be known as the Argonauts and would travel between Iolkos and Colchis in the greatest naval adventure ever told."

Nick paused and rubbed his beard. "And this is where we'll end the story of Jason."

"So, you're only going to tell me this part?" I asked, feeling a bit disappointed.

"That's right. That's what we'll discuss today."

"So, what does this story mean?"

"The departure is a critical step; without it, there would be no story." He chuckled. "You see, the departure is what sets the plot in motion. And this is worth considering, Andy." He paused to make sure I was following. "You see, a story—and our own personal stories, for that matter—are written with actions, so it's only when we get going that our story begins. You might have a bunch of dreams about the future and even some elaborate plans, but until you actually start pursuing them, there's no story to tell. No action, no story."

"That makes sense," I said. "What else?"

"Well, in the first act, the hero must symbolically cross a threshold. In Jason's case, this happens when he crosses the river Anauros, carrying Hera on his back."

"That's when he loses his sandal, isn't it?"

"That's right. In myth, crossing a threshold is a metaphor. It represents a transition from the ordinary world, in which the hero lives out his daily routines, to the heroic world, in which the quest will take place. Some mythographers believe the episode of the sandal represents instability as Jason takes his first steps in a world he's unfamiliar with."

I nodded.

"However," continued Nick, "what I find particularly interesting about this is the following: by crossing the river and losing his sandal, Jason becomes the man of the prophecy. Think about it. King Pelias was warned about a man wearing only one sandal. But that man, symbolically speaking, didn't really exist until Jason's sandal got washed away by the current. In that sense, crossing the threshold is what makes the hero the center of the story. The hero becomes 'the one' or 'the one whom the prophecy has spoken of.'"

"And what's all this about the ordinary world and the heroic world?"

"The ordinary world is usually the path we're already on; it's what's familiar and known to us. Today we might call it a comfort zone, and in that sense, crossing the threshold is like stepping out of one's comfort zone."

We both remained silent for a while. I leaned back on

my deck chair and stared at the sky, connecting one star with another, forming zigzags and loops. *My path led me to Grimshaw, to my inheritance. I would take over some day, like a prince who eventually becomes the king. But if that was the path I was already on, didn't it make it the "ordinary world" Nick was talking about? The world I would have to leave behind?* I shook the idea off.

"What else?" I asked.

"Well," said Nick, "now comes the important part."

I scoffed.

"I'm being serious."

I knew he was.

"Think about it for a moment. Why did Jason set off for Iolkos in the first place? What was on his mind as he crossed the threshold?"

"He wanted to be king, right? He was the rightful heir."

"Exactly!" said Nick with a big smile. He was enjoying himself. "But then he set sail on the *Argo*. Where was he heading?"

"He was heading to the end of the world to get the sheepskin."

Nick still had a half-smile on his face.

"You see, dear Andy, at the start of the story, heroes usually want something. But what they want is not always what they need. Jason wanted to be king, but his heroic path took him in a completely different direction. His quest took him to what he really needed, whether he knew it or not."

"I'm not sure I understand," I said.

"Well, this happens quite often in hero stories," he said, still smiling. "The heroic path takes heroes in a direction that seems contrary to obtaining what they want. It takes them away from their goals and is even seen as a distraction and a nuisance, something they need to get over with in order to get back on track. But this couldn't be farther from the truth. You see what I mean? Jason wants to be king, and yet his quest takes him to the end of the world to obtain the Golden Fleece, which is a symbol of legitimate rule and power. It represents the ability to be king, the wisdom to rule, and the experience to lead. All these things are what Jason needs before he can even think about becoming a king."

Nick stared at me, and I couldn't quite read his expression. It felt as if he was trying to tell me something. Then it clicked.

"You're saying that my visit to Arcadia," I said, "me being here instead of starting my internship at Grimshaw, is my heroic quest? That makes no sense." I was grinning in disbelief, waiting for him to deny it. He didn't.

I'm here to help you with the yard, I thought, *to pull prickly vines, of all things. There's nothing heroic about any of this.*

CHAPTER 13

THE NEXT MORNING, I woke up to a nagging feeling, a little tug in the back of my mind. It was faint but persistent, and I couldn't quite shake it off. And so it lingered, hanging around in the background and resurfacing in moments of quiet, like a soft whispering.

Nick had said something that struck a chord. Heroes, he had explained, leave behind what's familiar and head in a new direction, which often seems contrary to obtaining what they want, like a distraction or something that takes them off track. He seemed to suggest that my life in Chicago was this "ordinary world," as he had called it. My visit to Arcadia, by that logic, was some sort of quest to find what I truly needed. Nick neither confirmed nor denied this, but it sure seemed like he was trying to tell me something.

"Don't let the old man put funny ideas in your head," my mother had said. "You've been warned."

It was a silly idea, and I should have laughed it off, but for some reason I couldn't get it out of my head.

We went through our coffee routine in silence. Nick seemed to notice there was something on my mind, but he asked no questions and went about his morning routine as usual.

I resolved to stick to my original plan and get to work, hoping a more pragmatic mindset would shake off any distractions. I had one week left to help Nick with the yard, to set him up in such a way that he could manage without me. Then I would get on with my internship and shine in my new role. I would ace all my mother's assignments and prove myself a worthy heir to Grimshaw.

We suited up after coffee, and I worked with silent resolve. The goal for the day was to clear the second and third flights of stone steps, a rather ambitious target but well worth the effort. Once that was done, if the tractor parts arrived in time, we would be in good shape to clear the overgrowth and comply with the township's demands just in time for me to return to Chicago.

We worked in silence. I was on my knees, bending over the vines that covered the stone steps. I knew by then that different types of vines required different tools, so I alternated between the serrated sickle, the anvil lopper, and the weed puller. One after the other, the vines came out in long strings, which I piled beside me. Nick was working quietly behind me, using the pitchfork to stack the pulled vines into heaps.

By midmorning, the sun was blazing and a suffocating mist rose from the saturated soil. I was parched and soaked with sweat. I needed a break, and I craved fresh lemonade. Maybe it was time to sit down in the shade with Nick for a while.

I turned around to suggest my plan, just in time to see him tumble to one side and hit the ground with a thud. He just lay there, very still, carving his silhouette into the thick vegetation.

"Nick!" I called out as I scrambled toward him.

"Nick!" I yelled again and removed his sun hat and shook him gently. His face was gray and his lips were white, blending with his beard. I patted his cheeks and used my body to shield him from the sun.

"Nick!" I shook him again, and he blinked and groaned and coughed.

As he shuffled, I managed to pull him up gently and slide my leg under his head as a cushion.

"Nick?" His eyes blinked again and moved, but each one was pointing in a different direction. I patted his cheeks, and he slowly came to, mumbling and cursing.

"Let's get you inside, and I'll call 911."

"No," he muttered and made a feeble attempt to grab my shirt. "No."

I sat him up slowly, and after a wobbly moment, he was able to hold himself upright.

"Can you stand if I help you up?"

He nodded, or rather his head bobbed in a shaky diagonal.

"Okay. One. Two. Three." I grunted as I pulled him up. He wavered, and I wrapped his right arm around my shoulder to stabilize him.

"I'm fine," he said, suddenly annoyed, but then his head sagged and I felt his weight pull me down.

"Come on, Nick."

We inched forward toward the house. At times, Nick walked on his own and all I had to do was steer him. At others, he would go limp and I would have to spread my legs to hold myself up under his weight.

Once in the house, I laid him on the couch and brought him a glass of water.

"I told you I had my days," he said in a hoarse whisper. He was looking a bit better.

"I'll call an ambulance," I said, but he gripped my wrist with surprising strength.

"No. Snopengaard will see. Don't do it. I'm fine. I just need to rest."

"I don't give a shit about Snopengaard!"

He tightened his grip on my wrist.

"Alright. Alright," I conceded. "What can I get you? How can I help?"

"My pills. In the bathroom. Pill organizer. Give me the ones for today midday."

I rushed to his bathroom and immediately found what I was looking for: a plastic box with rows of flip-top compartments, each labeled with a day of the week and a time of day. It sounded like a maraca when I lifted it, pills shaking in their small containers.

As I turned to leave, I caught a glimpse of a colored leaflet resting on the far end of the vanity. It had a photograph of an older man that resembled Nick. The man in the leaflet was smiling, looking straight at the camera, radiating confidence. The face seemed to be nodding, a self-assured endorsement of some product.

Below the image, a black speech bubble shaped like a banner read: *Hormone therapy has kept my prostate cancer under control for five years.* Further down over a white surface in a clean, scientific typeface was a section titled "Questions and Answers about Your Prostate Cancer."

My breath became shallow as my eyes floated over the text. It said things about hormone injections and radiotherapy. The footnote showed the company logo in bright colors.

Courtyard Therapeutics. Your partner in health.

I returned to the living room a moment later, still in a shocked daze.

"What's this?" I demanded, holding up the leaflet.

"Oh… that…" said Nick and looked away.

"You have cancer?" My own words bounced around in my skull. "That's why you've been having those bad mornings?"

Nick waved dismissively and shook his head. He had recovered some of his color and was sitting upright.

"I'm fine," he said, still waving his hand.

I must have had a hard expression on my face because he hurried to continue as soon as our eyes met.

"Some mornings I wake up feeling like I haven't slept in years. That's true. But it's under control. You don't need to worry."

"Have you seen a doctor about this?"

"Yes, of course I have. I'm seeing Dr. Patil at Jackson. She said the fatigue is caused by the therapy. Really."

I looked away and heaved a sigh. I couldn't wrap my head around the whole thing. Nick seemed to think I was skeptical.

"I'm fine," he insisted. "I promise. You'll see. I'll be up and about again in no time."

"The hell you will. You'll stay in bed. That's what you'll do."

"You mustn't tell your father," said Nick, after a brief silence. "It'll just worry him, and he'll bring up the whole idea of me moving to Bradwick. And that snake I have for a neighbor mustn't know either. He'll tell your father if he knows."

"This is crazy, Nick. You can't keep this a secret. What's

gotten into you?" I said, but I could see his point. My father wouldn't be open to exploring other solutions for Nick's predicament. He would simply insist on Nick moving to Bradwick and leaving his beloved home behind. It made me angry, and I wished things were different.

"Alright," I said after considering my options. "If we're not telling him, then I'm in charge. We're going to see your doctor. Now."

Nick didn't protest, and soon we were merging onto the highway, heading to the Jackson Cancer Care and Medical Center in Harrisburg.

It turned out Nick was right, at least partially.

They checked his vitals and all seemed to be in order. Nick's oncologist went over his chart and asked him some questions. She seemed pleased, which came as a surprise to me. Apparently, Nick was responding well to the cancer treatment. The episode, she concluded, was most likely a side effect of the radiotherapy. Nick would have to be careful and take it easy. Any strenuous exercise like yard work, especially under the blazing sun, was strictly forbidden.

When we were all done, I walked alone to the parked car. The discharge procedure required me to pull up to the main entrance, where Nick would be wheeled up to the curb. He was not happy with the arrangement and protested, arguing he was perfectly capable of walking.

The sun was still high and had been shining on the car for the last hour. Even the air inside was scorching hot. I would have to cool it down before I went for Nick. I welcomed the pause and sat on the curb in the shade of a myrtle while I let the engine run with the air-conditioning on.

Dr. Patil's statements had been reassuring, but I was still in shock. Nick was being treated for cancer. That was the bottom line. And it changed things. It also explained a lot: Nick's inability to keep the yard under control, his occasional drives into Harrisburg, and his frail state in the mornings.

And furthermore, despite his apparent confidence, Nick was surely aware of the implications this had. *What point was there in fixing the yard and getting the tractor parts if he was too sick to take care of it by himself?* Snopengaard would only have more reasons for being a nuisance and my father would insist on him moving.

And then it dawned on me that perhaps this was the reason he had called me in the first place. Maybe all he wanted was to reconnect before… before it was too late.

When we were back at the house and I had helped Nick get into bed, I called Sally. She seemed happy to hear from me but soon realized there was trouble in my voice. I made her promise to keep our conversation secret and then told her about Nick and his illness. I told her all that had happened, from Nick fainting in the yard to the leaflet with information about prostate cancer I had found in his bathroom.

And then, I'm not sure why, I told her everything. Everything I could think of. Whatever crossed my mind. I talked about my summers in Arcadia, about Mimi and how I had been absent in her last moments. I told her about my mother and her endless lists of reading materials, about all the expectations around my internship and the LPS Conference. I told her about the Greek heroes and how Nick's stories always had some mysterious meaning. I even told her about serrated sickles and scythes and about the right way to pull a wineberry. The more I talked, the lighter I felt.

Sally listened patiently and encouraged me to go on.

"Oh no… I'm so sorry to hear that. Yes, I remember that. You mean, he tells you stories of Greek heroes? Which ones? A scythe? What, are you living in the middle ages?" And so on while I vented whatever was on my mind, shaping words out of random thoughts.

"I'll come over as soon as I get out of work," she said when I had finished.

⤝

The sun was going down when she arrived, and we sat on the wicker couch on the deck. The air was crisp and clear, as if the sun had dried any remaining moisture from the storm. Thin wispy clouds covered most of the sky, red and pink, like scales on a bright fish.

"What an amazing view," said Sally as she looked around in wonder.

I agreed. The whole valley was tinted red and blue and looked alien, like a strange paradise on a faraway planet. It struck me that nature never seemed to be concerned or moved in any way by our problems. It just "was," majestic and indifferent.

"So, how's Nick?" she asked. "And how are you?"

The breeze tousled her hair, blowing some strands across her face and prompting her to tuck them gently behind her ear. She was wearing a thin white blouse and blue pants, and it occurred to me that she looked great in any outfit.

"I'm fine, I guess. The whole thing was a bit of a shock. We were working on those steps, down there." I pointed and Sally followed with her eyes. "To see him sprawled like that in the tall grass… His face was gray and white. For a moment I thought he was…"

"But it's under control, right? His cancer, I mean," said Sally.

"It seems that way"—I nodded—"but you know doctors; they're so cautious. What she actually said, in medical jargon, is that you never know how things will play out."

Sally nodded and we both looked out at the forest. The red was dissipating, and the blue was taking over as the sky grew darker.

"Here's the thing," I said. "Nick is old. And he lives alone in this house. And he's sick. Even if he gets better from cancer, his situation isn't good. I mean, how much longer can he manage by himself? I'm not sure what to do. I only have one week left before I'm expected in Chicago. If I leave, it would be like abandoning him in a time of need. If I stay…"

"What?" asked Sally.

"It'll sound silly. You don't know my mother."

"Try me. I don't know her, but I know *about* her," she said.

"Well, with her, everything is a test. And if I bungle the internship and the conference, it would…" I tried to put my finger on exactly what the consequences would be. "I think it would make it harder to prove to her that I'm ready to take on more responsibilities at the firm."

Our arms grazed. Her skin was warm and soft, and I held on to the feeling as I looked out at the valley and pretended nothing had happened.

"It sounds a little harsh to me," said Sally, bumping her shoulder against mine. "Maybe you're taking this too seriously."

We remained silent for a while. Maybe Sally was right.

"I, for one, wouldn't mind if you stayed," she said with a mischievous grin.

Her voice had changed. It was softer and deeper. All of a sudden, I became aware of how close she was, her warmth filling the narrow gap between us. In the dim light, her skin looked so smooth it made me want to reach out and feel it.

"You're always so serious," she teased. "Always thinking about things."

She was right. And she was not the first one to tell me so. Maybe I did think about things too much.

"See? That's exactly what I'm talking about!" She slapped my shoulder. "You just did it again. You frown and your eyes wander away!"

I laughed, and it felt like a gentle ripple that loosened my shoulders. Her eyes glimmered. They were sharp and strong, but they had a dreamy quality as well.

"What?"

"You're just…" I said, stumbling over the words.

I swallowed, trying to breathe.

"What?" she asked and held my gaze.

Our eyes locked and our faces were so close I could feel her warmth on my cheeks.

I kissed her and she kissed me back.

Her lips felt soft and full against mine.

CHAPTER 14

I WOKE TO a bright, sunlit room. It took me a few yawns and stretches to get my bearings, and as soon as I did, I was overcome by a strange delight, a serene exultation, the feeling that everything was suddenly right with the world. I could sense the warmth and fragrance of Sally's skin, and I closed my eyes, allowing them to take over.

I reached over, but the bed was empty. *Had she taken off already? Had she gone to work?* Then I remembered it was Sunday and the world was supposed to run a little slower.

I strained my ears and soon heard muffled voices coming from the kitchen. Sally's giggles floated through the walls, and Nick's chuckles came in response. The two of them seemed to get along, which for some reason wasn't surprising.

I dressed and made my way to the kitchen, where Nick and Sally were drinking coffee. Nick still looked frail, but his eyes sparkled and he was cheerful. He sat at the kitchen table in his robe, his thin white hair standing straight on one side. Sally stared at me from above her mug as she wrapped it in both hands. Her eyes flickered playfully as if she and I were the only ones privy to some wondrous secret.

"Well," said Nick, looking first at me and then at Sally, "I will leave you two lovebirds alone so that you may enjoy each other's company. Sick old men have no business around young love."

I blushed and protested. Sally protested as well, but she didn't seem to mind as much as I did. In fact, she found the whole thing quite amusing.

The next few days were bright and sunny. Nick spent most of his time in the house, resting in bed or reading in his study. He looked better. His eyes were alert, and he spoke with his habitual enthusiasm. The thought of his cancer diagnosis and the strong impression it had made on me faded quickly. It was, after all, under control, and as long as Nick rested and kept away from strenuous activity, the side effects of the therapy would be manageable.

I decided I would stick to the plan and put all my energy into Nick's yard so that it could meet the township requirements by the end of the week. The tractor parts were scheduled for delivery by the following Saturday, just in time to get everything mowed down before I left. That would get Snopengaard off Nick's back—at least for a while—and would ease my father's concerns. I knew it wasn't a perfect solution, but it was the best I could do for the moment.

I removed the vines that covered the last flight of stone steps, trimmed the azaleas, and even dismantled the old raised beds in his vegetable garden, which had rotted and were short of collapsing.

Then there was the matter of the waste: large heaps of grass and vines beside the steps and along the footpaths we had mowed with the scythes. Some of the piles were relatively small and could be moved in three or four trips with the wheelbarrow. Others towered in stacks three feet high. One by one, I loaded the heaps and moved them to the border of the forest. By midweek, I had completed most of the work.

My Grimshaw homework was also in good shape, and I hadn't heard from my mother in several days. I thought maybe she'd run out of material for me to read, but then I remembered she'd flown to California and was probably held in back-to-back meetings with private equity fund managers. I couldn't say I missed her.

In the evenings, Sally would drive over after work and we would spend time together. We would take walks around the Collinsworth Estate and follow the main road through Laurel Hill until the stars came out. We would have dinner on the deck and listen to the sounds of the woodland. In the mornings, we would wake up in each other's warmth and I would make us coffee before she drove off to work again.

Nick insisted on giving us space and—to my dismay and Sally's amusement—kept calling us "lovebirds." But despite his insistence, we did spend some time with him too. We talked about Arcadia and its history, about Nick's teaching career and his life with Mimi. There was no shortage of topics.

Some subjects, however, we tacitly agreed to avoid. Nick's cancer was one of them. We would ask how he was feeling, and he would provide only a superficial—and humorous—report. Another forbidden topic was Nick's situation in Arcadia, and how things would work out for him over time, whether he could or could not manage the place by himself.

My imminent departure was probably the most tightly guarded topic, of which not even a hint was uttered. Ironically, it was the most palpable thing on our minds. Sally and I had become so close, I couldn't imagine us apart, even though we both knew that my return to Chicago was only days away. It made my heart feel heavy.

She felt something similar, I suspected. On occasions I would catch her brooding and she would pretend it was nothing if I asked, or she would joke about some random topic—mostly at my expense—to shake the subject off. Nick also kept up his cheerful tone, but I caught him looking at me once or twice as if he wanted to retain an image of my face in his memory.

I would check on Nick regularly and was vigilant with his medicine, making sure he took it at the right times. On Wednesday afternoon, I took a break from the vines and went inside the house to see how he was doing. He was resting in his room, reading a book.

"Are you okay? Do you need some water?" I asked.

Nick groaned and nodded. "That would be nice."

I helped him sit up, and he drank the whole glass.

"So, how are you feeling? What's up with you? And what are you reading?" I asked.

Nick chuckled. "I'm bored if you have to know. And most of the time, I'm just daydreaming." He looked at the book in his hands. "I'm only staring at this one. I can't seem to concentrate."

"Is there anything I can do?"

He was looking at me in a strange way as if he was

considering something. Then he sat straight, pushing himself up with his arms, and puffed the pillow behind his back.

"Since you're offering," he said, "I wonder if you would be so kind as to bring a book from my study."

"Sure," I said. "Which one?"

"The small green one you found in my library. The one titled *Heroikos*."

I returned moments later with the book in my hand. I had found it on the couch, still lying where I had left it. It was a strange book by all accounts, and I flipped through the pages before I handed it over to Nick. *Heroikos* read the cover in golden letters.

"The other day," he began, still looking at the book, "I noticed something when we discussed the story of Jason."

"What?" I asked.

"Something I said about the first act, about leaving behind the ordinary world and going on a quest that seemed contrary to the original goals, as if it was a detour from the plan."

I had forgotten all about it. The thought had nagged at me, that was true, but after all that happened, the whole idea seemed unreal, like a strange dream. It sounded childish and silly.

I nodded and he nodded in response.

"Look," he said, "I didn't mean to imply that I know what your path in life should be or what your journey is all about. How could I? I have no idea what lies ahead for me, so how can I tell what lies ahead for you?"

"But you're telling me these hero stories for a reason, aren't you?"

Nick thought for a while and then stretched out his arm, handing me the green book.

"Take a look, will you?"

I sat on a chair and flipped through the pages of *Heroikos*, stopping to read a few lines here and there. There were only two characters in the story, and they engaged in a long conversation about Greek heroes. Each entry was marked by the name of the character as in a movie script. The sentence would start with the word *Phoenician* followed by a colon and then whatever the Phoenician said. The next sentence would start with the word *Vinedresser* followed by a colon and then whatever the vinedresser said.

"And you said a vinedresser was like a gardener, right?" I asked Nick.

"Yes," said Nick. He pushed himself up again, sitting straight with his back against the headboard. "In *Heroikos*, the vinedresser plays two roles. On one hand, he takes care of the grave site of a great hero. Now, this particular grave site wasn't a simple plot in a cemetery with a common headstone. It was a large field with trees and plants. And the whole area was carefully landscaped. You see, it was sacred ground. So, in this sense, the vinedresser's duties were those of a groundskeeper, someone who spends most of his time keeping the place tidy by removing unwanted growth. Pulling out weeds and vines, if you prefer."

He winked at me.

"Hey!" I said. "That's what we're doing in your yard!"

Nick nodded.

"But this vinedresser wasn't just a simple gardener. He was doing much more than pulling vines. He was also performing acts of devotion, which were part of the hero's cult. Heroes were worshipped back then, you know, and their sacred rituals were carried out at their burial sites."

He paused and I remained silent, sensing something else was coming.

"The vinedresser, in other words, was also preserving the memory and honor of the hero. He was the guardian of the hero's legacy, and it was his job to keep it alive. His mission was to ensure that those willing to listen to the sacred stories could partake in the heroic tradition."

He gave me a meaningful look.

"So, what about these stories?" I asked.

"In *Heroikos*"—he pointed at the book—"the two men appear to be talking about the heroes of the Trojan War. But as they do, the Phoenician merchant crosses a mental threshold that connects him to the realm of heroes."

I remained silent, thinking about that for a moment. Then Nick continued.

"Remember when we discussed the nature and power of stories. I told you that as we experience them, we undergo a deep mental process. In this case, the Phoenician is also going through a mental process. He is becoming 'storied,' and by doing so, he undergoes his own initiation into the realm of heroes."

Something was beginning to make sense, as if soft waves of realization were lapping on the shores of my mind.

"We've been doing something similar," he continued. "Not only pulling the vines in the sacred garden but also talking about the heroes, discussing them just as the vinedresser and the Phoenician did."

"So, you're saying that simply by discussing these stories, I have also gone through some sort of… What did you call it? Initiation? Because I don't really feel any different if I have to be honest."

"Whether you realize it now or over time," he said, "you are also being 'storied.' A seed is being planted in your mind and in your heart. Now it just needs to grow."

Something fluttered in my stomach as if I was standing on a ledge. Even as my rational mind resisted the whole idea, another part of me was certain that after these few weeks in Arcadia, I would never see things the same way again.

"An initiation is like a mental connection. In this case, it's a connection with the heroic essence."

"So, all these stories of heroes are what? A guide for us to follow?" I asked.

"Something like that," said Nick, nodding.

"But why are you telling me all this?"

"Well, dear Andy, I am the vinedresser—figuratively speaking, of course." Nick chuckled. "And I must pass on what I know before I die."

CHAPTER 15

ON THURSDAY NIGHT, with only two days left before I had to return, the three of us had dinner on the deck. The air was warm after a hot, sunny day, and the breeze was but a whisper.

"Hey, Nick," said Sally when we had finished, "Andy tells me you have these great hero stories. Won't you tell us one?"

"Why not?" he said. "But you'll have to tell me what's on your mind, Miss Higgins, so I can pick the right one for you."

Sally was thoughtful for a while. She looked at me briefly and then turned to Nick. "Do you have one about a hero who has to make a decision whether to stay and stick it out or leave and get on with his life?"

Nick's eyes lit up. He liked the idea. I, on the other hand, felt put on the spot. Sally, in a clever way, had brought up the topic we had avoided all those days. Would I leave for Chicago and get on with my life, or would I stay a bit longer in Arcadia? But the idea of staying was absurd. *Stay and do what? Mow the lawn and pull weeds? Be the groundskeeper of a sacred site? That was nonsense. I had to get on with my life.*

Deep down, I really wanted to stay. I wanted to be with Sally. In fact, I would count the hours of the day to see her. But even if I did stay, she would return to Harrisburg at the end of summer, and I would have wasted a great career opportunity. Furthermore, staying would anger my mother and could even derail my future at Grimshaw.

Sally and Nick were both staring at me.

"Sure," I said, shaking away my thoughts. "Fine with me."

"Alright then," said Nick, holding a finger in the air. "I have just the one for you, and as it turns out, it also happens to be a good way to continue the conversation I've been having with Andy. You see, we've been discussing the hero's journey. We've covered the first act, which is called 'Departure.' Now we must discuss the second act or 'Initiation.'"

Sally gave me a funny look and shrugged as she grinned. I was serious, however. I knew I was being "storied," and that felt important for some reason. Besides, I was intrigued. *How would a hero decide whether to stay or return home?*

Nick rubbed his beard.

"You see, Sally, the second act is a turning point for heroes; it's the moment at which they fully commit to being the hero in their own story."

Sally stared wide-eyed at Nick.

"And before they can embrace their path," continued Nick, "heroes must go through a difficult ordeal, also known as the 'dark night of the soul.'"

"That doesn't sound very promising," I whispered.

Nick chuckled softly.

"I'll tell you a story about Achilles, who was the greatest hero of all, the best of the Greeks."

"Yes," nodded Sally. "Let's hear it."

"Okay." Nick tapped his fingers on the table. "From a very young age, Achilles excelled at everything he did. He was the fastest runner in his time and also a great orator, a fine singer, and a master of the lyre. He is most remembered, however, for being the very best warrior the world had ever seen.

"Achilles fought in the Trojan War. He commanded a fleet of fifty ships and a battalion of mighty warriors known as the Myrmidons. He was joined by Patroklos, who was his best friend and right hand, his most trusted adviser and closest companion.

"During the tenth year of the war, after the Greeks had sacked and destroyed all the kingdoms surrounding Troy, Achilles fell into a bitter dispute with Agamemnon, who was the king of Mycenae and the leader of the Greek campaign. The argument enraged Achilles so much that he swore to withdraw from battle and hold his Myrmidons back, knowing his absence would turn the tables and bring disaster upon the Greeks."

Nick paused for a moment and frowned, considering what to say next.

"Did they? Did the tables turn against the Greeks?" asked Sally, urging him to continue.

"They did, indeed. The Trojans, led by Prince Hector, took advantage of Achilles's absence and pressed forward. Clash after clash, they forced the Greeks to retreat until the fighting had almost reached their camp by the ships. After ten years of fighting and in just a matter of days, all seemed lost.

"King Agamemnon was desperate. He realized it was time to make amends with Achilles and try to persuade him to rejoin the battle. He decided to apologize and shower him with presents and treasures, hoping he would change his mind."

"I have a feeling Achilles won't budge so easily," I said.

"You're quite right," said Nick. "Achilles was no ordinary man, and he wouldn't be easily appeased. And Agamemnon knew this, so he chose three men to deliver his peace offering. He picked Ajax, who was Achilles's cousin; Odysseus, who was known for his wise counsel; and Old Phoenix, who was Achilles's foster father. These three men were probably the only ones Achilles would listen to. They were his best chance.

"And so, the three men made their way in the dark of night, reaching the tent of Achilles, and found him and Patroklos playing the lyre and singing songs about great heroes. Odysseus took the lead and spoke of the amends Agamemnon was willing to make. He listed the many treasures and war prizes Achilles would receive if he stayed at Troy and continued fighting."

"But Achilles said 'no,' right?" asked Sally.

"Correct. Achilles rejected the offer. But something had changed in him. He wasn't angry anymore. His mood had become somber, maybe even sad. You see, Achilles was struggling inside, trying to make up his mind about something important.

"The men remained silent as Achilles stared into the fire, lost in his thoughts. After a while, he looked up and spoke to them in a soft voice. This is what he told them:

"'Long ago, my mother foretold this moment and spoke to me about my destiny. She said the day would come for me to choose between two fates. If I return home to my dear land, I am fated to live a long and prosperous life until the time of my peaceful death, upon which my name will vanish from memory. On the other hand, if I stay and fight, I will die at the walls of this city but will gain eternal glory and men will sing my name for thousands of years…'

"The messengers looked at each other, disconcerted, unable to understand what he meant by these strange words."

Sally and I also exchanged glances, and I felt a strange numbness in my temples as if the words of Achilles held some momentous significance in my own life.

"'Tell Agamemnon,' Achilles said, standing and concluding the meeting, 'that I have no intention of fighting until the Trojans are at my tent, setting the ships on fire. Only then will I rejoin the battle.'"

Nick sighed and remained silent for a moment.

"So, what happened then?" asked Sally.

"Well, the next morning the battle resumed and the Trojans gained ground once again, getting closer and closer to the Greek ships until they managed to set one of them on fire. Just to be clear, fire on the ships was the worst nightmare for the Greeks; it was the unequivocal sign of doom. Without their ships, you see, they would never be able to return home.

"As the Greek soldiers saw the dark smoke rising in the air, their hearts dropped and they all asked themselves the same question: 'What is it all for? The whole ten years of siege, the toil and the effort, the blood and the sweat, the death and the lamentations? We suffer all these things, and all that awaits us at the end is death.'

The situation was so desperate that Patroklos begged Achilles to change his mind and lead the Myrmidons into battle."

"And this time he did, right?" asked Sally.

"Well. Not exactly. Patroklos proposed a plan, a sort of compromise. 'Let me, glorious Achilles, wear your armor and helmet and lead the Myrmidons into battle. Our comrades will believe it is you, and they will find courage in their hearts,' he said.

"This was a good idea, in fact. The crisis at the ships would be averted, and Achilles would stay true to his oath. But Achilles was worried about his dear friend and hesitant about sending him into battle.

"Patroklos insisted and eventually got his way. He led the Myrmidons into battle, storming the beach like a swarm of angry wasps. The Trojans paled with fear when they saw the armor of Achilles, and their battalions began to retreat, trampling over each other in their haste. In a matter of minutes, Patroklos and the Myrmidons had cleared the skirmish by the burning ship and extinguished the fire.

"But instead of returning to camp after his success, Patroklos pressed on, overtaken by blood lust and rage. He sped across the plain all the way to the gates of Troy, where he met Prince Hector and faced him in single combat. The two heroes fought fiercely and hacked at each other with their swords. In the end, Hector would be the one to deliver the final blow."

"He killed him?" gasped Sally. Her eyes shone in the soft light.

Nick nodded. "Hector killed Patroklos and took his armor—Achilles's armor—as a trophy."

Sally's expression was serious.

"Back at the Greek encampment," Nick continued, "the news reached Achilles like a deadly lightning bolt. He was so struck with grief when he heard about his dear friend that he made a low, growling moan, chilling the blood of those around him. 'This senseless war has brought me nothing but loss and disappointment,' he cried. 'What is it all for anyway, when death is the fate of all men?'

"He was so stricken by sorrow that he wandered aimlessly along the beach, at times staring into the sea through his tears and at others pacing and moaning like a madman. He sobbed bitterly until his despair was slowly replaced by a heaving rage and an overwhelming desire for revenge.

"The next day, the Greeks advanced once again with the support of the Myrmidons. But this time, it was Achilles who led them."

"So, he chose to stay," I said under my breath, sensing more darkness ahead.

Nick nodded. "Yes, Achilles chose to stay and fight. He managed to push the enemy battalions back, forcing them to retreat all the way to the city. Eventually, he came face-to-face with Hector and, after a bloody combat, killed him with his sword."

We were all silent for a while. The breeze had picked up, and Sally and I put our arms around each other for warmth.

"So, what happened next?" I asked.

Nick patted his thighs.

"Well, this is where we must end this story."

"But you will tell us more, right?" asked Sally. "Like… what happened to Achilles?"

"Well… When all the funerary rites for Patroklos

had been performed and the mourning period was over, the war efforts resumed. Achilles, at that point, had fully embraced his path. He had chosen to stay and fight at the walls of Troy, forsaking his return to Phthia and his home on Mount Pelion. He would never have a family of his own, nor a household filled with memories. He would never experience old age and would never know peace. All that remained for him was to die a glorious death in battle."

"So, he dies in the end?" asked Sally. "I thought... I thought the prophecy might change... or something..."

She was quiet for a while, and I suspected the story wasn't quite what she had hoped for. I squeezed her closer to me, and she rested her head on my shoulder.

"So, what does this one mean?" I asked. "It's kind of dark..."

Nick nodded.

"It certainly is," he said. "And it's also complicated and mysterious. Keep in mind that I've only told you a short and very simplified version of this story."

"So, what's his decision about really?" I asked. "I have a feeling it's more than just a choice between staying and leaving."

Nick rubbed his beard. "Achilles must pick one of two paths, both of which are precious and important. He can choose to return home and live a long and prosperous life in anonymity, or he can stay and die a glorious death in battle and be remembered forever."

The trees swayed and hushed in the darkness as the breeze picked up, and Sally shivered and pressed herself against me.

"An interesting thing about this story is that, right now, more than three thousand years later, we are still talking about Achilles. We remember his name, and we speak of his deeds, and by doing so, we are fulfilling the prophecy and becoming part of his myth."

I was reminded of what Nick had said about the power of stories. Achilles seemed to live on in a strange dimension, stepping beyond the boundaries of his own myth, his spirit living among us whenever we uttered his name.

"But," I said as I put my thoughts together, "did he really choose? I mean, if Patroklos hadn't died, the story would have been very different. It seems to me that Achilles wanted revenge."

"That's true," Nick nodded. "Achilles was certainly driven by revenge. And this is true in our own stories as well. We choose one path or another for a whole number of reasons. Ambition. Pride. Love. Most of the time, unfortunately, we're driven by fear, which stops us in our tracks and steers us away from the heroic path." He sighed and shrugged. "In any case, Achilles is driven by more than revenge. Remember, I told you that heroes must go through a difficult ordeal before they embrace their path."

"Yes," said Sally. "What's that?"

"Well," said Nick, "you can think of it as a profound experience, something that marks a turning point in the story. At its core, this ordeal is a representation of death, which heroes must experience in some way before they can get on with their journey."

"Why death?" asked Sally.

"Because, dear Sally, the realization of death puts our life in perspective. It forces the existential question on us. You see, Achilles is deciding what kind of life is worth living in the face of inevitable death."

"That's heavy," I said, shaking my head.

Nick nodded and chuckled.

"Anyway, the ordeal can be represented in many different ways. In some stories, the heroes have a close encounter with death and barely survive. Sometimes, they actually die and somehow come back to life. In other cases, it's represented symbolically, when heroes go underwater or climb down into a dark cave. And in many cases"—Nick raised a finger—"the ordeal is represented by the death of someone very close to the hero."

"Patroklos," whispered Sally.

"Bingo," said Nick. "Achilles faces his ordeal when Patroklos is killed. It's his darkest hour, the point at which he comes face-to-face with loss and with the notion of his own mortality."

"So, what's up with Patroklos and Achilles?" asked Sally. "Were they lovers or something?"

Nick seemed to consider this for a moment. "You have to remember that these are mythological characters; all we know about them is what we're told in their stories. Sometimes we project our imagination onto them and shape them this way or that. Some see them as friends. Others see them as lovers. But, in terms of the deeper meaning of this myth, none of that might even matter."

"What do you mean?"

"Well…" Nick smiled and looked around. "There's no easy way to put this, so I'll just say it. Patroklos and Achilles seem be two representations of the same self."

"What?" I asked. "You're saying that they were the same person?"

Sally's eyes opened wide, and Nick chuckled softly.

"I didn't say they were the same person. I said that they might be two representations of the same 'self.'"

"Like an alter ego?" I suggested.

"Yes… something like that. Some mythographers describe Patroklos as Achilles's second self, which is equally enigmatic."

I shrugged. "So, what does that mean?"

"It means that when Patroklos dies," said Nick, "it's like a part of Achilles has died."

I sighed heavily, blowing out my cheeks. Sally was shaking her head.

Nick smiled and looked out into the dark valley. In the distance, the lights of Harrisburg glowed softly.

"The second act, or 'Initiation,'" continued Nick, "is a process of deep personal transformation. This means that a part of us must die—metaphorically speaking—so that a new self can emerge."

Metaphorically speaking or not, I thought, *having a part of me die is not something I'm looking forward to.*

CHAPTER 16

SALLY DROVE OFF the next morning, and I waved good-bye from the front porch. We hadn't said much as we sipped our coffees. We hadn't slept well either. We both tossed and turned, and our dreams were troubled, full of things unsaid.

It was Friday. The tractor parts were scheduled to arrive in the afternoon, and once the lawn was mowed and all was set, I would leave for Chicago. I had reserved my flight for Saturday night, and I toyed with the idea of bumping it to Sunday so I could spend another night with Sally. My mother would freak out, but that was okay, I reasoned. After all, if she didn't freak out about that, she would about something else.

I was still sipping my coffee on the front porch when I heard a soft metallic clank. I looked up just in time to see Snopengaard close Nick's mailbox and start back toward his house. I remained as still as I could and watched. I was pretty sure he hadn't seen me, but just as he passed in front of where I sat, he nodded and smiled.

I raised my hand but said nothing.

As soon as he was back in his house, I walked to the

mailbox, flipped it open, and retrieved the correspondence. Two blue envelopes were stamped *3rd Notice* and *Repeat Violation* in bold red letters. There was a third envelope. It was bright white and larger than the other two. The stamp on it read *Court Summons*.

As I stared down at the envelopes, I got the distinct impression that Snopengaard was peeping from a window, monitoring my reactions, maybe even relishing the moment. I looked in the direction of his house, raised the letters, and waved them, forcing a defiant smile. I could almost swear that, as soon as I did this, there was a flutter in the kitchen window.

❧

Nick read the letters in silence, shuffling the papers and reading them over and over again. His eyebrows met in a frown, and his forehead was lined with furrows.

"What do they say?" I asked.

He mumbled some of their content as he read them a third time.

"Due to inability or defiance… homeowner has failed to fully comply with remediation efforts in accordance with citations for overgrowth and fire hazard… established deadline…"

He continued reading from the next letter.

"Failure to comply… repeat violations… identified during inspection…"

"What inspection?" I demanded. "There was none!"

He went on reading without looking up.

"Increased penalties… fines and fees… cumulative and escalating penalties as determined by township authorities… homeowner is willfully ignoring municipal regulations and creating a public nuisance… actions leading to a formal public complaint…"

He read the third and final letter.

"Legal proceedings… court summons… homeowners are required to appear before the judge… repeated violations and failure to comply with municipal codes… contempt of court… if the homeowner continues to resist or fails to appear in court… fines… resulting in a jail sentence…"

A part of me was expecting Nick to chuckle and make one of his funny remarks or even find a clever way to make fun of Snopengaard. But when he looked up, he was pale and disoriented. He looked so frail and vulnerable that my heart sank.

"It's all a lie!" I said. "We'll just tell them it's all Snopengaard's doing."

Nick shook his head. "We're past that now. This is a court summons. Snopengaard probably has photos of the yard and whatever else he needs to make a case against me."

"But the inspection," I insisted. "That never happened. That's a lie!"

"Are you sure about that?" He shook his head. "When he came over with the flashlight that night… He's smart in his own ugly way. But none of that matters now. At this point, calling him a liar would only make things worse for me."

"This can't be happening," I said. "What do we do now?"

"No, young man. There's no 'we' in this. You'll return to Chicago and get on with your life. That's what you'll do." He smiled, but there was pain in his eyes. "You've helped a lot, Andy, more than you can imagine. Now, it's time for you to move on."

❦

Later that afternoon, after Sally had finished work, she and I strolled around the Collinsworth Estate and took the nature trail across the open field, heading toward the north end of Laurel Hill. There was still plenty of daylight, but the trees around us cast long shadows. We held hands and our shoulders rubbed and bounced off each other as we walked.

I had shown Sally the township letters, hoping she would dismiss the whole thing. Maybe it was some sort of misunderstanding. But she said nothing as she read, frowning and shaking her head.

"I'm still shocked by the letters from the township," I said. "What the hell does that Snopengaard want?"

"I know, right? There's something strange about them," she said. "I've seen situations escalate, mostly in the Harrisburg office, but nothing like this. Failure to comply is one thing, and I can see why Nick might get multiple citations for the overgrowth. Chuck can be a jerk, and even more so when he believes he is doing the right thing, but the whole fire hazard allegation... and the formal complaints about Nick willfully ignoring regulations... It just seems too much."

I heaved a sigh.

"I don't know. I have a bad feeling about this," continued Sally. "Chuck must be up to something."

"I wonder what the beef is between Nick and him," I said. "Why would he do something like this? Think about it. He's going through a lot of trouble himself, just to make Nick's life miserable. And then he brings my father in, telling him that it's better for Nick to move."

Sally hummed in agreement.

By the time we reached the edge of the woodland, the sun had gone down behind us and the forest looked ominous in the dusk. We decided to cross the bridge over the creek and take the quiet lane that bent around the other side of the Collinsworth Estate and connected back to the main road.

"It's such a bummer I have to leave," I said.

"Well… that's your choice, Achilles," said Sally, bumping softly into me.

"Yeah…" I said as I thought about it, "but if I stay, a part of me would have to die… so no thanks."

"I wonder what part of you would die?" she said and grabbed my arm. "Would it be this part? Or this one?" She tickled me and laughed and then put her arms around me. "You're such a dork, Romano. You know?"

I had no idea what part of me would die if I chose to stay, but I certainly felt I would lose something if I left. I would lose Sally and her beautiful face. I thought I'd say this to her, and then I changed my mind.

"I know," I said.

We walked up the main road toward Nick's house as the last light dimmed in the west. We remained silent the rest of the way, but Sally held my hand and squeezed it every now and then.

By the time we turned off the main road onto Nick's street, the night had closed in. Every single light in Snopengaard's house was on, flooding his end of the street. Beyond, there was only darkness.

I had a bad feeling.

"Nick hasn't turned on his lights," I said. "That's not like him."

"Maybe he's napping," said Sally, but her voice was uneasy.

I ran to the house, and Sally followed behind me.

"Nick!" I yelled as I clambered up the stairs. The house was in complete darkness. "Nick!"

I reached his room and flicked the switch. Nick was in his bed. He'd been sitting up against the headboard and had slumped over, his head hanging above his knees. He was very still, and his skin was gray.

"I'll call an ambulance," I heard Sally say behind me.

"Andrew Romano?"

It was a man's voice.

I was sitting on a plastic bench, mounted to the wall of a long hallway, lit from above by white fluorescent tubes. My elbows rested on my knees, and my head hung forward as I stared at the floor. I had been in that position for a while, and I felt a tingling in my feet and knees. Sally was sitting beside me, stiff and upright. She hadn't moved a muscle.

The ambulance had brought us to Harrisburg Central Hospital, and the paramedics had immediately rolled Nick to the emergency room. Sally and I were guided to a reception area, where they asked me a bunch of questions and had me sign some forms. Then they pointed to the hallway and asked us to wait.

We'd been sitting there for a couple of hours.

"Mr. Romano?" the voice asked again, and I looked up. "Hi, I'm Nurse Kowalski," said the man.

He was dressed in light blue scrubs and wore a mask over his mouth and nose.

"Are you Andrew Romano? You brought in Nicholas Romano, is that correct?"

"Yes," I said after clearing my throat.

"Are there any other family members with you, Andrew?" He looked at Sally.

"No…. Yes…. Sally is a friend of the family. Wait. How's Nick? Is he alright?"

"Right now, he's stable," said Kowalski. "But we're running a few tests to see what's going on. We've contacted his oncologist, Dr. Patil, and she's providing some input as well."

"But what happened to him? Is it serious?" I insisted.

"We don't know yet."

"Can I see him?" I asked.

"I'm afraid not. He's in the critical care unit. He's unconscious but breathing on his own."

Kowalski tried to reassure me when he saw my expression. "Look. It could be something simple, like electrolyte imbalance. He's in good care, and we're monitoring him closely. I would suggest you go home and try to get some rest. Nothing will change between now and tomorrow morning, and someone will call you if anything does."

I stared at the floor again.

Before Kowalski could leave, another voice came from the hallway.

"Andy?"

My father was rushing through the hallway toward us. Behind him, Karl Snopengaard was doing his best to catch up. He moved like an ostrich, bobbing his head back and forth while he marched in long, gawky strides, holding on to his eyeglasses with both hands so they wouldn't slip off.

My father looked at me and then at Sally.

"Mr. Snopengaard called me when he saw the ambulance. I came as fast as I could." He was out of breath, and his thin gray hair was messy as if he'd been rubbing it or scratching his head. He reminded me of Nick.

"George Romano," he said, stretching his hand out to Kowalski, who repeated all he had said to me.

"What do you mean 'cancer treatment'?" he asked, quite alarmed, as soon as Kowalski had finished his report.

"Mr. Romano has early-stage prostate cancer and is being treated by Dr. Patil at Jackson Cancer Care. Now, if you'd excuse me, I need to get to other patients," he said and left.

"Did you know about this?" asked my father.

I looked away. I knew I was guilty, but I didn't have the energy to argue with him.

"When were you planning on telling me? That wasn't the responsible thing to do, Andy. I am his son, and I am your father. What the hell were you thinking?"

My shoulders grew heavy, and I felt a weight pulling my arms down. I thought, for a moment, that I should put up a fight. I had been the one taking care of Nick, after all. When I arrived in Arcadia, Nick was by himself, dealing with his problems as best he could. I had put in hours of hard work. I had shared evenings with him. I had cheered him up. *Where had* he *been all that time?*

"It's a long story," was all I answered. "And it's been a long day."

To my surprise, he wrapped his arms around me and squeezed me. I didn't know how to respond, and my arms went limp, hanging by my sides.

"I wish you had told me," he said, releasing me. "I know how much you care about him and, even if you don't always agree with me, I also want what's best for him. You know?"

"So do I," jumped in Snopengaard, adjusting his glasses. "I also want what's best for Nicholas, and I had no idea *whatsoever* about his condition."

"Haven't you done enough, Snopengaard?" I snarled. "What are you even doing here?"

"Well… I…" Snopengaard stuttered. "If you have to know, I called your father as soon as I saw the ambulance. It was the right thing to do. That's what good neighbors do."

"And what about the notices you left in our mailbox? Is that your idea of being a good neighbor? You know, Nick was really upset when he read what you sent. I think what happened to him"—I looked around to signal the hospital—"has to do with your little letters."

"What are you talking about, Andy?" asked my father. "What letters?"

I remembered what Nick had said as he read them. Snopengaard had surely documented his case. Calling him a liar wouldn't help; in fact, it would only make things worse. Again, I felt my shoulders sag and a sense of defeat in my stomach. I realized there was no point in arguing or making a fool of myself in the hospital hallway.

Snopengaard jumped in to answer the question. "I'm afraid, George, as I told you on the phone, Nicholas has incurred some minor violations to our municipal code. Nothing serious, of course. But, well"—he coughed and his glasses slid down his nose again—"despite several notifications that were sent to him, he has, I'm afraid, failed to comply. You know how these things are. There's a process. I'm afraid once citations have been made, there are steps to follow. Township regulations."

He started coughing, and I thought he was going to have a fit. Then he managed to compose himself and adjusted his glasses again. "There are now fines and fees to be paid. And Nicholas will have to appear before a judge. I did all I could to prevent this from happening. But you must understand, I have a duty."

Small beads of sweat had appeared around his temples and forehead, and he looked oozy.

Sally was staring at me, raising her eyebrows, trying to tell me something, something about Snopengaard.

He's lying, she mouthed.

"Well, thanks for all your help, Snopengaard. You're certainly a good neighbor," I snarled again.

"I'm sure we'll be able to sort it out," said my father, instinctively putting his arm between me and Snopengaard.

Sally also jumped in and put her hands gently on Snopengaard's shoulders. "Come, Chuck. Why don't we get some coffee? Andy and his father surely have things to discuss. Family matters. I saw a coffee machine around the corner in the next hallway."

"I don't want any coffee," said Snopengaard. "I'm fine."

"Chuck," insisted Sally, "let's give them some space, shall we?"

She steered him away from us, turning his shoulders in the direction of the coffee machine. Snopengaard looked confused and a bit flustered but eventually complied.

"What's all this business between you and Mr. Snopengaard?" asked my father when we were alone.

"Snopengaard is not who he pretends to be," I said. My tone was flat and dispassionate as I spoke. I felt exhausted and impotent. "He's been harassing Nick while he pretends to help. He's up to something. I know it."

We sat side by side on the long bench.

"I guess none of that matters anymore," I said after a while. "If Nick… When Nick gets better… What I'm saying is that I see your point now. Nick shouldn't be living in that house all by himself, given his condition. He'll have to move. I understand that now."

He patted my shoulder. I said nothing, but that simple gesture had a strange effect on me. It reminded me of the weight I had been carrying and, at the same time, it took some of it off. I realized, with some surprise, I was happy my father was there beside me.

Eventually, Sally and Snopengaard made their way toward us, walking slowly along the hallway. She had a cup in each hand, and she offered one to me and one to my father.

"I'm Sally, by the way," she said, "Sally Higgins."

"Of course!" said my father. "You're Bernie's daughter! My goodness. Last time I saw you, you were a little girl." He shook his head and smiled. "It's nice to see you again, Sally."

There was something different about my father, but I couldn't put my finger on what it was. He had changed in some strange way. Or maybe I had.

"Any news?" Snopengaard stuck his head into our little circle.

"No," said my father. He gave Snopengaard a meaning-ful look. "But we need to talk. Let's get together early next week, Karl, and discuss what to do about Nick's house. I think we've reached that fork in the road. It's time for him to move."

Snopengaard couldn't hide his delight, and his mouth contorted as he tried to restrain a smile.

"Now we should get some sleep," continued my father. "There's nothing else to do here."

Indeed… I thought, *there's nothing else to do here. And Nick…* I looked down the corridor again and my stomach turned. *I failed him.*

CHAPTER 17

IT WAS A long, sleepless night.

I stared at the ceiling most of the time, tormented by worries and stubborn thoughts, seized by dread and sorrow and distress. I felt hollow inside, as if sadness had burrowed a hole in my chest. It was something I had never experienced before, a sense of helplessness and the certainty that all was lost.

Sally slept beside me with one arm over my chest and I kept still, trying not to disturb her. I could feel her breath on my shoulder and found some solace in it, but not enough. I just lay there as the hours went by, unable to stop thinking or steer the voices in my head.

Of all possible scenarios, the worst one had played out. I had gone to Arcadia thinking I would make a difference. I was confident I would fix things for Nick and, in doing so, atone for my absence during Mimi's last days. I would make the world right again and return triumphant to Chicago and set myself up to become the heir to Grimshaw.

How painfully naive.

As things stood, Nick was in the hospital fighting for his life, and even if he recovered, it had become clear he would still have to move. He would have to leave his beloved house behind, filled with the memories of a lifetime.

It just broke my heart.

Meanwhile, I had wasted two precious weeks of my internship and would be at a serious disadvantage, forced to catch up for the planning conference. And that was only if I flew back the next day, which I wouldn't. There was no way I would leave Arcadia under the circumstances. I had to stay a few more days, at least until things sorted themselves out.

Sally shuffled and winced in her sleep, and I stroked her arm until her breath became steady again. She looked so beautiful in the dim light; her skin was smooth and soft, and her honey-colored hair was tousled over the pillow.

I would lose her as well. We belonged in different worlds.

I had never felt so sad.

At daybreak, I sat on the porch with my steaming coffee. Heavy, gray clouds rolled southward, indifferent to the world below. I noticed two large cardboard boxes stacked in the corner on the other side of the front door. They were the tractor parts.

I scoffed at the irony.

What use are they now? I thought. *I should give them to Snopengaard, so he can sell them together with the house.*

My father joined me a moment later, sipping his coffee.

"I was just on the phone with the hospital," he said. "Dad's been in and out all night. They say he has a serious infection, and they're giving him antibiotics. Apparently, the cancer treatment lowered his defenses."

"Will he be alright?"

My father shrugged.

"I asked the same thing. They told me that at his age and in his condition, it's hard to tell. They said if he responds to the antibiotics, things could improve."

We sat there in silence for a while, staring at the distance. I followed one cloud after the next, tracing their trajectory across the gray sky. I was absorbed with the vastness of the scene, the sheer scale of the world. Our stories seemed so fleeting, our actions so futile.

"I thought I'd make a difference," I said with a sigh. "I thought I'd save the day... be the hero or something like that. And I thought I'd prove you wrong, you know? I wanted to show you that Nick was fine here, and there was no need for him to move."

"You have a good heart, Andy," he said. "And you did all this for the right reasons."

I shook my head. "What good has it done?"

"Listen, Andy, I can assure you that coming out here and spending time with Nick has meant a great deal to him. It's been a blessing, in fact. And I can tell you—without a doubt—that you've made a difference. And a big one."

"When Mimi was ill," I said after a while, "I didn't do anything. I pushed the thought of her away and pretended nothing was happening. Mimi had surely wanted to see me, but I was too busy with things I thought were more important. I never forgave myself for that. I vowed not to repeat that mistake. That's why I came."

I'd never talked about this with anyone and, as soon as I'd finished, a strange feeling took over me, a buzz in my arms and legs that slowly moved to my temples. My own words echoed in my head as if repeating themselves might underscore their importance.

"It seems you've been carrying a heavy weight for a long time," said my father and shook his head. "You were just a kid, Andy. You dealt with things the best you could, and you shouldn't beat yourself up like that. In fact"—he raised his finger as he said this and he reminded me of Nick—"now you know better. And that's why you're doing things differently. That's what growing up is all about."

He even sounded like Nick.

The buzz intensified and moved to my belly and chest.

We sipped our coffee in silence, and I thought of all the summers I had spent with my grandparents. The thought of Mimi took front and center until I could almost see her smiling. I had always found comfort in her. She had been warm and patient with me that first day when I was dropped off in Arcadia, the time my father left me with that huge suitcase.

I looked at him and I had the same impression I'd had the night before. He was different in some way. And as the clouds continued to fly past us, I realized I had been angry at him long enough, and that none of that mattered anymore. Perhaps it never had.

"Remember that day," I said, not quite sure where the words were coming from, "when you dropped me off here for the first time? That summer you and Mom needed to 'figure things out'?"

He nodded.

I told him how I remembered the episode and how I'd been angry at him.

"It doesn't really matter anymore," I said. "And it's a

silly thing, I guess. Life is complicated, and sometimes things just happen the way they happen."

My father's face was pale as he stared straight forward, gripping his mug. He was very still for a while, his eyes flashing.

"It was your mother who packed that suitcase for you," he said after a while. "And she packed another one for me, if you have to know. She had planned the whole thing to the last detail."

I tensed up.

He explained that my mother had asked *him* for a divorce, not the other way around. She had, quite clinically, explained that she needed to move on, she was not mad at him, she was not seeing anyone behind his back, and she had no ill will against him or his family. She just… needed to get on with her plans, and my father wasn't in them.

"I was shocked," he said, "and there was nothing I could do or say to make her change her mind. You know how she is. She had some sort of plan. I suppose she had started to envision Grimshaw Realty and I didn't quite fit in that picture. I guess I'll never know."

He sighed and shook his head.

"But from my perspective," he continued, "my world was suddenly on its head. I mean, our marriage wasn't perfect. Nobody's is. And I just thought Margaret's distance would blow over and we'd be fine. I just… It all came as a surprise. I didn't know up from down."

Instinct forced me to keep very still. A part of me knew something important was happening, like a revelation from an oracle or something like that.

"You never told me," I whispered. I wasn't really

demanding an explanation; I was just signaling my igno-
rance on the matter. I had been kept in the dark about this
most of my life.

"Of course, I never told you." His face relaxed a bit.
"When you were a kid, you were too young to understand,
and it wouldn't have been fair to expose you to all the nas-
tiness. Then the years went by, and Margaret took you
to Chicago, and you turned into an angry teenager who
wouldn't talk to me."

He made a face and broke into a smile. There was
something redeeming about it. I took a deep breath and
something seemed to dislodge in my chest and was released
as I breathed out. I realized it had been my mother, rather
than him, who had kept these things from me.

Before I could say anything, he continued.

"Look, Andy," he said. His voice was troubled again.
"I've made many mistakes. Sometimes I wish I could go
back in time, you know? Fix things. Or change them in one
way or another. But I can't. I just can't. All I can say is that
I've always loved you… And I'm sorry."

A stupid tear rolled down my cheek, and I looked away
and cleared my throat.

"So, what's your plan?" he asked after a few moments.
"Are you leaving today?"

"No," I said and wiped my face without him noticing.
"I'll stay here for now, at least until Nick wakes up… and
we can get things more or less sorted out."

"What will your mother say? I know you have that
internship thing."

"She'll be pissed," I said with a defeated smile, "but
what can I do?"

"Your mother… She means well—in her own

way—but she always has plans, and she doesn't want anything getting in their way."

The clouds became patchy, and a brief opening bathed us in sunlight.

"If you're around Margaret long enough," he said thoughtfully, almost to himself, "you may end up being a character in her story."

⋧

The buzz was still in my body long after we ended our conversation. I decided to take a walk to clear my head. My plan was to cross the Collinsworth Estate and take the trail by the creek, deep into the woods.

You were just a kid, the words bounced about in my head. *You dealt with things the best you could. It was your mother who packed that suitcase for you. And she packed another one for me, if you have to know. I've always loved you… and I'm sorry.*

The sky was slowly opening up. More and more sunlight would pour through the clouds, making everything bright. Then it would retreat, dimming the world once again.

As I passed in front of Snopengaard's house, I noticed two pickup trucks parked on his driveway, which seemed unusual. The one closer to the street had a sign on the driver's door.

Jonathan Morris

Land Surveyor

When I reached the corner and the Collinsworth Estate came into view, I saw a group of men in the distance, standing on the far end of the property where the forest began, which was the highest point on the hilly terrain.

They were far away, but I was able to count four figures. They were huddled around a yellow device, like a tripod, and took turns looking through a camera or a small telescope. They were looking at another man, standing in the opposite corner of the field, holding a tall pole.

I decided to continue down the road until I reached the forest and make my way through the trees until I was closer to them. I wanted to remain undetected, so I walked carefully and stayed on the trail to avoid snapping branches or ruffling the vegetation.

Eventually, I got close enough and was able to see them more clearly and even hear some of their conversation. Snopengaard was among the men, which didn't surprise me. He moved back and forth and fidgeted constantly, adjusting his glasses and looking around.

The voices were muffled, but I could pick up a few phrases here and there. One of the men hunched over and looked through the lens.

"You'll get better density if you rotate the lot lines fifteen degrees. It'll cut less into the slope," he said.

Snopengaard nodded and approached the lens to take a look himself as if to validate what the man had said.

"Yes," he said, "Fifteen degrees."

The wind picked up, swaying the trees, and the men's voices were drowned by the rustling sound of the leaves. They seemed to be discussing something, exchanging ideas. They pointed across the field and drew lines in the air with their fingers. One of them shook his head and pointed in the opposite direction.

Now and then, I managed to hear a few phrases.

"… keep the lots perpendicular to the main road… avoid adding a new cul-de-sac…" one of them said.

Another man shook his head.

"… stormwater basin. We can use that natural swale…"

"… turn it into a retention pond…" said another.

"… that would be nice… bump up lot prices…" said the first man.

I had to get closer.

I moved slowly, testing the ground with my feet before putting my weight down. As I approached the edge of the forest, the vegetation thinned and I felt more exposed. I squatted and pushed my way through the bushes until I was just a few yards away from them.

"We're looking at eighteen quarter-acre lots if we use a single access design and add the pond to the lower end," said one of the men as he folded the tripod.

"Twenty," said Snopengaard.

I inched forward to see their faces, and the branch I was holding snapped. The four men looked in my direction and I froze. For a moment, none of us moved. I held my breath, paralyzed with fear, my heart beating out of my chest. Snopengaard squinted into the bushes. He looked nervous and moved his head, trying to see between the leaves.

"You were saying?" asked one of the men.

Snopengaard was still looking in my direction. I could have sworn our eyes met.

"Mr. Snopengaard," said the man again, "you were saying?"

"Yes. Yes. I said twenty. Twenty lots, not eighteen. But we'll discuss that later on. Let's get back to the house now." He walked a few steps behind the men, and just when I thought the danger had passed, he stopped and turned around. He squinted again as he looked in my direction and placed his hand on his forehead to shield his eyes from the sun.

I held my breath.

After a while, he turned away and hurried toward the group, making his funny strides with his head bobbing back and forth.

"Hey!" he said, holding on to his glasses. "Wait up."

What are you up to, Snopengaard?

CHAPTER 18

"HOW DID YOU find everything?" asked my mother as soon as she picked up the phone. "I haven't been home in over a week.

She's been on the West Coast, I remembered. *That's why she hasn't noticed yet.*

"I'm not in Chicago, Mom."

"What do you mean? Are you hurt? Where are you?"

"I'm not hurt, Mom. I'm in Arcadia."

There was a long silence.

"Let me be as clear as I possibly can," she said. "You need to get yourself on a plane immediately and be at the office on Monday morning for the drill. The spotlight will be on you, so you better be ready. Monday morning. Not Tuesday. Not Wednesday. Monday. Is this clear enough for you?"

"Nick is in the hospital. I won't leave until I'm sure he's alright."

"What happened? How is he?"

"He has a serious infection. He's in the ICU. We still don't know if he'll make it."

"I'm sorry to hear that. And where's your father?"

"He's here in Arcadia. He arrived last night."

"Listen, Andy. I know you care about Nicholas, but your father should be the one taking care of this, not you. There's nothing you can do there."

"I won't leave, Mom. Not yet."

There was another long silence.

"You don't seem to understand the situation. I have already announced you will be representing Grimshaw at the planning conference. You are expected. This isn't just about you; it's about Grimshaw and how we're perceived by our stakeholders. You will be taking on increasing responsibility at the firm. If you don't show up, if you're not well prepared, if you fumble this in any way… the board will notice. The community will notice."

"I'm sorry," I said. "I didn't mean any of this to happen."

"Andy, there's too much at stake. You realize I'll have to replace you if I have any reason to believe the plan is compromised, don't you?"

I thought about my father and the suitcases. He had been replaced when he was no longer part of her plan.

"I'll be there as soon as I can, Mom. But it won't be Monday. It'll be later in the week. I'll do everything I can."

"This ship is sailing, Andy. With or without you," she said and hung up.

⌁

"Maybe Collinsworth finally decided to subdivide his land after all these years," said my father.

We were driving to the hospital. They had called to say Nick was awake. He had responded well to the course of antibiotics, and we were allowed to visit.

"That might be it," said Sally. "He's rich. He lives in New York. He doesn't even visit Arcadia as often as he used to."

"Exactly," said my father. "He has no use for the land anymore."

"Or maybe," said Sally with wide eyes, "maybe he's dead. Maybe his heirs have decided to cut up the estate and sell the lots. Maybe they're fighting over the scraps, trying to get a bigger slice, plotting schemes."

"Yeah, but where does Snopengaard fit in all this?" I asked.

Sally seemed disappointed at my skepticism.

"Well," she said, "if you have to get all serious about everything, here's what I think. Chuck is the township manager. Maybe Collinsworth—or his heirs—asked him to oversee the subdivision and deal with the land surveyors and all the paperwork. In a small town like Arcadia that would be perfectly normal."

"Still, something doesn't add up," I said. "Who would buy the lots? Everybody seems to be leaving town. According to Snopengaard, selling Nick's house will be very hard and we won't even get a decent price for it. If the same logic applies, it should also be hard to sell all that land."

"You're such a buzzkill," said Sally.

"How many lots are there in total?" asked my father.

"It was hard to hear clearly," I said, "but they were talking about eighteen-quarter or twenty-quarter acre lots."

"That means twenty families wanting to build a home in Laurel Hill," said my father. "It sounds unlikely."

"Snopengaard is up to something," I said. "Remember how happy he was when you told him we would sell Nick's house? What if he's made an offer for the Collinsworth Estate?"

"That doesn't make any sense, numb nuts," said Sally. "According to your own logic, he wouldn't have anyone to sell the lots to. Besides, with what money would he make the offer? Not everybody is rich."

She stared at me with fiery eyes, and we held each other's gaze for a moment. She was so pretty, it hurt.

"Yeah," I said. "I guess you're right. But I still think Snopengaard is up to something. I don't like that guy."

"Really?" she said, punching my arm and making faces at me. "I hadn't noticed."

Our eyes met again, and for a moment, I thought I could see something in hers.

"If I had to bet," she continued as if nothing had happened, "I would say that all this is just one of Chuck's nonsense initiatives. He always has these dumb projects and makes a big fuss about them as if they were critical to the survival of the township. He's a weird guy. I'll give you that."

"That's probably the most logical explanation," I said, looking out the window. "Just Snopengaard being Snopengaard."

Nick had been placed in a private room with a window. It had a couch and a TV, on which he was watching the news. He was pale and a bit thinner but seemed to be in good spirits and even joked about his situation.

"So, when are they letting me out?" he asked, looking at us, one by one. "Have the tractor parts arrived?"

"Take it easy, Dad," said my father. "Yes, the parts arrived, and when they let you go, we'll get that tractor working again."

We talked about this and that but were careful to avoid certain topics. We had agreed, for example, not to discuss Nick's impending move to Bradwick. There would be time for that when he was better.

There was a small table beside the couch on which I was surprised to see another prostate cancer pamphlet, just like the one Nick had in his bathroom, with the gray-haired man in the photo and his confident smile.

"These materials," I read out loud, "are designed to empower prostate cancer patients with knowledge about their condition, treatment, and self-care, as well as to provide guidance on navigating the treatment journey effectively."

The pamphlet was designed in question-and-answer format. A light blue cartoon doctor, wearing glasses and a white coat, appeared several times on each page, using speech bubbles to answer a long list of questions.

"Hear this," I said. "Hi there—I'm Dr. Prost! I'm here to walk you through everything you need to know about prostate cancer, one step at a time. And listen to this: PSA stands for 'prostate-specific antigen,' but I like to think of it as 'please see a urologist.' Unbelievable. It goes on for pages and pages."

"Who even writes that crap?" asked Sally.

"Well…" I said, turning it over. The company logo and slogan were at the foot of the back page. "Courtyard Therapeutics. Your partner in health. They're based right here, in Harrisburg."

"Wait a second," said Sally, giving me a strange look. "Let me see."

I handed her the pamphlet.

"Yes. This is their logo, alright. Karl has been meeting with one of their executives."

"What for?"

She shrugged. "Nobody knows. Karl always keeps these things to himself. He hasn't involved me or anyone else at the office."

I inspected the pamphlet again and found a brief *About Us* section.

"It says here they make drug delivery systems for cancer treatments. Tubes and pumps and these weird-looking syringes."

"What could Karl possibly want from them?" asked Sally.

"I'm telling you, Snopengaard is up to something," I said.

"We should investigate," said Sally, biting her lower lip, "like in the movies. We need to get to the bottom of this. What do you say, Detective Romano?"

I scoffed. I had enough on my mind as things stood. I hated Snopengaard, but once we sold Nick's house, he would be out of my life. As much as I disliked him, he was not my problem.

Sally wasn't happy with my reluctance. Our eyes met once again. I was expecting her to make a face or something, but she just stared back at me.

"I'll go grab a coffee," said my father. "Anyone want something?"

I shook my head.

"I'll join you," said Sally, standing. "Talk to him, Nick," she said, pointing at me with her thumb. "He's frownier than usual."

"She's right," said Nick. "You look like you have a lot on your mind."

I scowled.

"Well? Are you going to tell me or what?"

"I don't know." I shrugged. I knew, of course. I knew Nick would have to sell his house. I knew I would lose Sally. And I knew I was compromising my future at Grimshaw. Maybe I already had…

"It's a long story. But I think I messed up my internship."

"You mean, by coming here to Arcadia? I'm so sorry to hear that. I hope I didn't cause you any trouble."

"No. It's not you, Nick," I said. "It's my mother. There's a lot at stake, or so she says. If I don't get back to Chicago soon, she'll go ahead without me." I shrugged. "She might even replace me with someone else. It will be hard for me to get on her good side again."

Nick nodded and made a face as if he knew what I was talking about.

"So, what are you going to do?"

"I don't know." I shrugged again, and my shoulders felt heavy. "How come the heroes in your stories always know what they're supposed to do? It's as if their paths are clear all along."

"Not for Achilles," said Nick. "That's why I told you his story."

I sighed and shook my head.

"Figuring out your path is a complicated process," continued Nick. "It takes time. In the second act, heroes begin to realize they are reaching the point of no return, but they still don't know exactly how things will play out."

"And when do they know? What else happens during the second act?"

"Hmm," he said. "Let's see. We already discussed the ordeal, the moment in the story when all seems lost, when heroes experience death in one way or another, and the world seems to turn against them."

I remembered I had spent a sleepless night tormented by thoughts of loss and the futility of my efforts.

"Let me think," he continued. "After the ordeal, heroes become whole again, and stronger, and are able to complete the mission and get their reward."

"That sounds a bit more promising."

"Oh, but there are stages in between, my dear Andy. There's also the atonement with the father."

"What did you just say?"

"I said *atonement with the father*."

I thought of the conversation I'd had with my father on the front porch.

"Do you mean the actual father of the hero?"

"Well," said Nick. "Only when heroes experience loss and defeat, when all seems lost, are they able to reconnect with their father figure. They tap into their personal history and rediscover their true identity. Sometimes they may even straighten out misconceptions about their own past. And once they go through this process, they become whole again—psychologically speaking, of course. It's at this point they become ready for the final stages of their journey."

"And what comes after that?" I urged.

He looked into my eyes with an elusive smile.

"Next comes the 'Apotheosis.'"

"Apotheosis?"

"Yes. Apotheosis. It means 'to become a god.'"

"To become a god," I repeated slowly.

"I know... It sounds a bit grandiose. You can think of it as a form of elevation, the moment heroes rise to the challenge and become their best self."

I nodded slowly as I tried to make sense of it all.

"Apotheosis," continued Nick, "is also a transcendent moment—like an enlightenment—in which heroes gain the insights that allow them to complete their quest."

I remained silent. I had nothing to say, and I wasn't even sure what question to ask next. A huge weight pulled my arms down.

"It seems to me," said Nick, "that it's time you figure out what your story is all about."

No kidding.

CHAPTER 19

IT WAS MONDAY. Sally was at work. My father was in Nick's study, correcting papers, and Nick was still in the hospital. A few more days, they said, until the infection receded.

I decided to take a walk and clear my head, maybe try to figure out what my story was all about. I thought I would take the usual path across the Collinsworth Estate but changed my mind at the last minute. I didn't want to run into Snopengaard and his crew again.

Instead, I went through the back door and across the yard toward the end of the property. The paths we had mowed with the scythes were still visible, but the grass had grown again over the course of the week. In just another week or so, there would be no traces of all our hard work. Hours of effort would disappear under new layers of green.

I descended the flights of stone steps, one terrace at a time, until I reached the edge of the woodland. I was sure I would remember the spot, the entry point to a barely trodden footpath leading to the trail that ran alongside the Whistana River.

A quick inspection of the border revealed nothing but thick vegetation—most of which was thorny—guarding the access to the woodland. A few failed efforts and several nasty scratches later, I finally located the footpath and began my way down into the valley, trekking through undisturbed forest and using the sound of the rushing Whistana as a compass.

I was in another world, dark and green. The ground was covered in moss and ferns and fallen trees. I could only see small patches of blue sky through the sparse openings in the canopy.

My story is all about Grimshaw and becoming the successor of my mother, I thought. This seemed plain and obvious, as it had been for years. But as I continued my way down the hill, it became clear there was more to it. *Maybe Arcadia is the detour that becomes the quest, after all. But I still can't see how.*

It took me longer than I remembered to reach the riverbank. It was hard to see my way clearly, and I found myself stopping every now and then, trying to get my bearings, looking for familiar stones or trees. The trail hadn't been used in a long time.

I realized, just before I caught a glimpse of the water, that the drill at Grimshaw would be starting about now. Mother would be overseeing the preparation of the talking points and following the planning conference schedule to establish goals for each interaction. I wondered if she had already chosen a replacement for me or if she had stalled and changed her plans until I returned. *Would she give me another chance?*

There was a lot at stake for her, I understood that. She was grooming me as her successor, and there would logically be a whole lot of attention on me. It was my duty to make her look good and strengthen the stakeholders' confidence in her judgment. She took these things very seriously, which was probably one of the reasons she was so successful. A painstaking obsession over detail. An unbreakable will to control everything.

I'm not sure I can be like her, I thought. And then another idea occurred to me. *I'm not sure I even want to.*

There was a small inlet where the river formed a gentle pool, surrounded by large boulders. Some of them were wet with spray and splashes as the river gushed against them. I picked a large stone at the downstream edge of the pool and sat there. The sun had been shining on it all morning, and it was warm and dry. I took off my shoes and dipped my feet in the cold water. The Whistana rushed by me, dashing against the stony banks and flowing steadily in the mid-channel, where it was deeper.

"If you're around Margaret long enough, you may end up being a character in her story," my father had said. *I don't want to be a character in her story. I want to be a character in my own story. In fact, I want to be the hero in my own story.*

A splash in the river startled me. It was a brown trout, as far as I could tell. It swam slowly into the pool where my feet dangled and looked for a shady spot where it stayed very still. I stared at it, waiting for it to move. Then it twitched and suddenly vanished.

I decided to continue downstream along the trail toward Harrisburg. The landscape changed quickly as I walked, and the sound of the Whistana grew to a roar. The valley became narrow and deep, and the banks became steeper, meeting the water at small cliffs, covered in bushes and brambles. I was at the gorge.

As I turned the bend, I was stopped by safety tape, tied to branches on either side.

The tape read: *Caution—Do not enter.*

I looked around, making sure I was alone. There didn't seem to be any danger, so I tugged the tape gently and slid beneath it, entering forbidden territory. I walked slowly, staying alert and listening for voices against the rushing water. At every turn of the path, I expected to see Snopengaard and his crew.

The trail narrowed to a thin ledge with the Whistana flowing on my left just a few yards below. Keeping my balance was tricky, and I was afraid I might trip on a root or a loose stone and fall. There were jagged rocks piled on both sides, and the current was strong enough to flush me away if I fell.

After a few minutes I reached an opening where the vegetation had been cleared. Some sort of measuring equipment had been set up, among which was the same tripod and small telescope I had seen the other day on the Collinsworth Estate. The area was cut off by safety tape, surrounding the equipment in a semicircle.

A sign read: *Township of Arcadia—No trespassing.*

What are you up to Snopengaard? I thought.

I hated that guy. I hated that he was up to some mischief I couldn't decipher. But as much as I disliked him and whatever business he was up to, it wasn't my problem. He—Snopengaard—wasn't my problem.

Stay focused on what's important, on your strategic priorities. All the rest is noise, I could hear my mother's voice.

Once Nick's house was sold, Snopengaard would be out of my life.

And so would Arcadia.

And Sally.

I hated him.

And then I realized Snopengaard *was* my problem.

He is very much my problem. He messed with Nick and that will not stand. He's up to no good and I know it. And knowing it makes the whole thing my problem.

I couldn't simply shrug it off. I had to do something about him.

⌁

"What made you change your mind?" asked Sally.

We were lying side by side, naked and relaxed. The afternoon air still felt muggy and hot, and I kept looking at the window, hoping the breeze would pick up, ruffle the curtains, and dry our bodies.

Sally shook my shoulder.

"Hmm?" I said.

"What made you change your mind?"

"Your pretty face."

"No, numb nuts. Really."

"I don't know," I said, stretching my arms and yawning. "Maybe I just hate Snopengaard."

Maybe I just love you too much and I'm looking for an excuse to stay here a bit longer, I thought.

"Maybe I always wanted to be a detective," I said instead.

"You're such a dummy." She cuddled beside me.

"I don't know, Sal. I guess I just liked your idea. To investigate. To get to the bottom of the whole thing and find out what Snopengaard is really up to."

"And what about your internship? Isn't Madame Grimshaw livid with rage at this point?"

I shrugged. She probably was.

She snuggled closer, and I put my arm around her. *I could stay here forever*, I thought, *in this room with the sound of the river rushing through the valley and Sally's warm skin against mine.*

"So, what do we do then? What's the plan?"

"We're going to break into Snopengaard's office," I said.

"Seriously?" She sat up, her eyes filled with worry and excitement. "And what if we get caught?"

"I'll just tell them it was your idea."

She punched me in the shoulder. "I'm being serious."

"I thought you wanted me to be Detective Romano. We'll be Romano and Higgins, Private Investigators. How's that?"

"And what are we looking for?"

"I'm not sure. But we'll know when we find it."

Arcadia's town square was deserted, except for the bar on the corner of Market Street and the convenience store at the gas station. I drove past the park and the township building and turned onto a side street. There was a dark spot a few blocks down where I parked Nick's Honda. I left the car unlocked and the keys in the ignition. If we had to run, there would be no risk of fumbling.

Sally had been quiet while I drove, and when I asked if she was ready, she only nodded. I guessed she was apprehensive, and I couldn't blame her. She only spoke again once we were inside the building.

"Don't use the flashlight yet," she said. "Stay close to me."

When we reached the mezzanine, she pushed the massive door that flanked the front desk. It made a hollow groan as the hinges rubbed and scraped under the weight, and I feared it would get us caught. We kept still for a moment, but the building was quiet and dark and unaware of our intrusion.

We felt our way through a labyrinth of desks and filing cabinets, turning one way and another across the office floor, until we reached the door in the opposite corner. It had a little sign that read *Karl Snopengaard, Township Manager*.

"Give me some light," she said as she unlocked the door. "I'll pull the shades so we can use his desk lamp."

It was a square office with tall windows on the street side and a high ceiling. A massive desk stood in the middle of the space, and a heavy black chair with a tall backrest was tucked beneath it. The opposite wall across the desk displayed a map of Arcadia. It had an antique, ornate frame.

"You check the desk. I'll take the flashlight to the archive and look for building permits and zoning forms. Maybe there's something there."

I sat at Snopengaard's desk. There wasn't much on it: a few forms neatly stacked in a letter tray, some papers right in front of me—presumably what he was working on before he left for the day—and a pencil holder crammed with blue pens, all identical. In the middle of the desk, opposite the chair and facing the door, was a walnut nameplate with Snopengaard's name on it.

I shuffled through the papers, but nothing caught my attention. There was a sturdy institutional brochure beneath the papers right in front of me. *Heritage Investment Group* was printed in large, formal type across the top of the brochure. I put it aside and went through the rest of the papers but found nothing. Beneath the stack was a weekly planner, and something in it made me stop and look more closely. Scribbled under *Wednesday* was the name Gregory Collinsworth and a phone number.

Sally came back into the office and closed the door behind her. She was holding a form.

"What did you find?" I asked.

"Not much." She shrugged. "But I thought this was interesting. It's a project proposal and estimate for the construction of a road, a new exit on the highway that would lead directly to Laurel Hill."

She looked above my head at the map of Arcadia and walked around the desk to get closer to it. There was a green section west of the town center between Laurel Hill and the highway. She traced a line with her finger, connecting both points. The Whistana River flowed between them.

"I saw township equipment by the Whistana Bank, just about here." I pointed at the map. "The road will need a bridge."

"This is a large-scale project," said Sally. "And there's been no talk about it as if Karl was keeping the whole thing to himself."

I traced my own finger across the map, starting from the point on the highway nearest Laurel Hill, passing through the narrow bend of the Whistana, where I had seen the equipment, and then toward the north, trying to keep the line as straight as possible.

"What on earth? See this?"

Sally got closer to see what I was pointing at. The line led straight into the Collinsworth Estate, passing right next to Snopengaard's house.

And Nick's.

"He must be planning some sort of residential development in Laurel Hill," I said. "With its own access to the highway."

"But why is he being so secretive? None of this is illegal," said Sally, "or wrong in any way. In fact, it would be good for the town."

"I'm telling you, Sal, he's up to something. Otherwise, there would be big announcements… meetings… I don't know… some sort of town hall."

I showed Sally the planner and pointed to Collinsworth's name.

"You think Collinsworth is in it too?" she asked.

"Could be."

I tried the drawer, but it was locked.

"Wait," said Sally. "The keys are always here." She took a key chain from one of the shelves by the door, unlocked the drawer, and began shuffling through papers.

The first thing she pulled out was a folder with plans and maps. *Jonathan Morris, Land Surveyor* was printed on the front. There were property boundary maps and topographic surveys. One read *Floodplain Certificate* and another was titled *Right-of-Way Map*. They all showed Laurel Hill and its surroundings, with the Collinsworth Estate in the middle of it all. The last map was titled *Subdivision Plat*. The Collinsworth property was crisscrossed with lines, forming roughly rectangular plots of about the same size. The road from the highway was marked as well, only instead of reaching the development in a straight line, it made a turn and went around the estate on the north side and looped back to reconnect with Redwood Road.

"That's strange," said Sally. She then counted the lots on the map. "Eighteen, just as you said."

"Twenty," I said. "That son of a bitch is including his own land, and Nick's, in the development. Look"—I pointed at the map—"Nick's house would be the largest lot, close to the main access. With the view of the valley, I'm pretty sure it would be the most expensive one as well."

"That's why Karl wants Nick's house so badly," said Sally, tapping her lips as she thought. "The letters Nick got in the mail," she muttered after a while, "you said Chuck put them in the mailbox himself?"

I nodded.

"At the hospital," she continued, "when he was explaining the citation process to your dad as if some complex machinery had been set in motion and he was unable to prevent it from escalating, he was lying. He could have delayed or stopped any of all that, if he wanted to. And the court summons… That's a bit drastic."

"What are you trying to tell me?" I asked.

"That the letters he left in Nick's mailbox are bogus. They have to be."

"Is there any record, like a ledger or something where these things are documented?" I asked.

We stepped out of Snopengaard's office and sat at Sally's desk. She logged in to her computer and accessed the township system. "Let me check the ledger. No, there's nothing here. That means—"

"That the accusations were fabricated, and the notices were falsified. They were just a form of intimidation, of bullying."

"It's more than that," whispered Sally, looking back at the screen. "It's a case of abuse of public office. There's also falsification of public records, fraud and harassment. And the fake court summons… That would be contempt of court." She looked up at me. "He could go to prison for a very long time."

A door slammed below us in the main lobby, and we both froze.

"Did you leave any door open?" I asked. "Maybe it was the wind."

Sally shut down the computer, dashed to Snopengaard's office to turn off the desk lamp, and dragged me behind a large cabinet in the opposite corner of the space. I thought she was overreacting but followed her just in case.

Then I heard the voices.

CHAPTER 20

"I STILL DON'T see why we need to meet at this time," said a man's voice, echoing from the empty lobby up to the mezzanine.

Sally and I kept still, crouched behind the cabinet, as the sound of approaching steps carried into the room. A few lights flickered on.

"What are we going to do?" whispered Sally.

There really wasn't much we could do, except stay still and hope we weren't discovered. I held my breath, trying to listen. There appeared to be two people, but it was hard to tell.

"I have a bad feeling about this," said the man's voice again. "This is so unusual. It's like we're sneaking around. This is not one of those money-laundering operations, is it?"

"Let me reassure you, Sam, if I may… that there's no reason *whatsoever* for any sort of concern."

It was Snopengaard. I felt the urge to spring out of my hiding place and knock him right off his feet. Sally put her hand on my shoulder and touched her lips, urging me to keep quiet.

"That's what you keep telling me, Karl, but all this is very… unusual."

"It's a perfectly legitimate operation."

The man scoffed. "You better be right about that."

"Let me remind you, Samuel," said Snopengaard, "that a traditional bank would demand all the paperwork up front and the whole project would be out in the open before we even got the money and secured the land. There's nothing illegal in what we're doing. It's only a matter of discretion. I saw the opportunity, and I won't be shouting about it from the rooftops. This town owes me enough already. And besides, Heritage Investment Group is a reputable enterprise. They deal in… venture capital."

The door slammed shut in the lobby.

"Hello?" A voice came from downstairs.

"We're up here," yelled Snopengaard. "Right up the stairs."

I peeped from behind the cabinet. The corner where we hid was still relatively dark, and I was quite sure they couldn't see me from where they stood. I moved very slowly just in case.

A third man joined them and nodded briefly to one and then the other.

"Mr. Dogrun," said Snopengaard. "Thank you for joining us."

The two men shook hands. Dogrun was stout and heavily built with a round face, big nose, and thick eyebrows. "Let me introduce you to Samuel Gross," continued Snopengaard, "vice president of operations, Courtyard Therapeutics. Sam, this is Mr. Ozgul Dogrun from Heritage Investment Group."

Both men shook hands. The guy from Courtyard

Therapeutics was tall and thin, similar in build to Snopengaard.

"Alright," said Dogrun in a thick accent. "Let's get down to it. What's the status?"

"Well," said Snopengaard, adjusting his glasses, "the land surveyors and engineers have documented the feasibility of both the bridge and the subdivision of the Collinsworth Estate. There should be no trouble getting those approved… once, of course, we are in possession of the property."

"What about the approval of the subdivision?"

"That, in fact"—Snopengaard adopted a more confident posture—"is the beauty of this. Old Collinsworth got the approval for a subdivision years ago, when all his neighbors cut up their land and created Laurel Hill. We don't need any paperwork for that. It's an interesting story, in fact." Snopengaard adjusted his glasses as he spoke. He had become excited.

"Yes, yes," Dogrun cut him off. "I get it. Has this Collins person accepted the verbal offer?"

"Yes. We're still ironing out a few details, but we've agreed on the price."

"Does he have any suspicions?"

"No," said Snopengaard. "He's got other priorities. This doesn't mean much to him anymore. In fact, he's surprised there even is an interested party."

"What about the other old man's house? The one down the street from yours."

Snopengaard looked around and adjusted his glasses. "The family has agreed to sell. The old man is in the hospital and will be moving out of Arcadia. I will buy the property—as agreed—and we'll include both my land and Romano's in the development. They will be prime spots."

Sally grabbed my arm again, seemingly afraid I would jump out of our hiding place and punch Snopengaard in the face.

"Okay, okay," said Dogrun. "It's twenty lots, including those two."

"Yes, the surveyor… well… we have the plans… I can… with his signature, of course."

"Yes. Yes. I'll take all the documents with me tonight. What about the bridge and the access to the highway?"

Snopengaard fidgeted with his hands, removed his glasses, and wiped his forehead. "That… well… Here's the thing. We won't get state or county funds for that without… exposing ourselves… our… enterprise. We've reassured the people at Courtyard that access is guaranteed. They… well…" He looked at Gross.

Dogrun gave Gross a deadpan stare that chilled my blood. He looked as if he was demanding an answer.

Gross cleared his throat.

"We have the green light from headquarters. We'll use one of the old factories as a research and materials testing facility for drug delivery systems. A small operation, but we'll offer relocation benefits to some of our employees."

"We're certain," rushed in Snopengaard, "that once Arcadia has one company opening shop on the old factory road and a few new families settling into Laurel Hill, then more will come."

Snopengaard's comment reminded me of the analysis I had carried out the previous week. Arcadia certainly had potential; it just needed a nudge in the right direction. It needed more than that, in fact, but Snopengaard was not entirely wrong.

"Besides," he continued, "the new access to the highway will cut the commute between Laurel Hill and Harrisburg by half. This is a safe bet."

Dogrun shifted his attention back to Snopengaard. "I saw the abandoned factories on my way here. It's a complete dump."

"Courtyard will be repurposing the old cork factory, the one with the Armstrong sign."

Dogrun shrugged. "They all look like crap to me."

"Well," said Snopengaard. His voice quivered. "I beg to differ. They are great buildings. They just need a little care."

Dogrun scoffed.

"Armstrong Cork is the brick building next to Bethlehem Steel. It's really beautiful, for a factory, I mean. It's got a lot of history."

Dogrun dismissed Snopengaard, waving his hand. "And Courtyard will be paying for the land remediation?"

"We have the assessment," Snopengaard hurried to clarify. "It's not that bad. Not bad at all."

There was a brief silence. Gross cleared his throat.

"So," he said. He seemed hesitant. "What kind of operation do you run, Mr. Dogrun? What are we looking at here?"

"What you're looking at is quite simple." He leaned toward Gross until their faces were very close. Gross became uncomfortable and took a step back, clearing his throat. "You want to leverage a situation, but you don't have the money. You can't go to the banks without disclosing your plans and exposing yourself to competing bids. So, we step in and take care of it and you don't ask questions."

Gross looked at Snopengaard.

"And how do I get my cut? I play a role in this. I've risked my job. I've moved things around."

"You'll get your cut. Just make sure you don't cause any trouble. It's not that hard. Just lay low for a while. We'll take it from here."

Gross was about to protest but then changed his mind. His shoulders sagged.

"Alright then," continued Dogrun, "give me all the documents. I'll hold on to them until we need them. And make sure you don't leave any paper trail. Get rid of everything. Everything," he repeated, looking at Snopengaard.

Sally and I exchanged glances. We needed those documents as evidence. The men proceeded to Snopengaard's office.

"Listen, Sal," I whispered. "We need to stop them."

Sally's eyes grew wide, and she shook her head.

"Move over to the desk." I pointed further down the corner. "Hide under it. I'll try to stop them, and we'll see how things go. We need all those papers and whatever they have on Snopengaard's computer."

She shook her head again and grabbed my hand.

"Trust me. It'll be fine."

She crawled on all fours toward the last desk in the room, looking over her shoulder every now and then. When she had settled in her new spot, I made my way to the opposite side, closer to the front desk. I still wasn't sure what to do, but my jaw was tight and my hands were curled into fists.

"That's enough, gentlemen," I said, standing. I was

close to the main entrance of the office as if I'd just arrived. There was no turning back now.

Snopengaard and Gross jumped and stared at me in panicked disbelief, their mouths gaping. Dogrun kept very still with his eyes locked on me, like a crouched predator, waiting for the right moment to attack.

"The police are on their way," I said, trying to sound convincing.

"Police?" asked Dogrun. "Whatever for? We are just talking business here. No crime. And who are you, may I ask?"

"I know what you're up to," I said. I'm not sure how I was expecting to thwart them, but there was no other way, so I pressed further. "And I know the police will be interested."

"Who is this person?" asked Dogrun. He directed his question at Gross and Snopengaard, who stared wide-eyed at me.

"Oh, for heaven's sake," he said as he unholstered a gun and pointed at me. Gross flinched and Snopengaard gasped and his glasses slid to the floor. The sight of the gun made the blood drain from my head, and I felt dizzy and strangely detached, like a witness to some parallel reality. I just stood there, numb with dread.

"Put that away," said Snopengaard as he stooped to pick up his glasses. "What are you doing?"

Dogrun ignored him.

"Stay right where you are, boy," he growled. "And keep your hands where I can see them."

Gross tried to make it to the door, but the gun cocked and he froze.

"Everybody needs to stay very calm," said Dogrun.

"Am I making myself clear? Nod if you understand me. Gross? Nod if you understand me."

Gross turned around and nodded, his face contorting into a mask of horror. Snopengaard heaved, and I thought he would faint.

"For the third time, who is this?" asked Dogrun.

There was silence.

"Snopengaard!" barked Dogrun, seeing he was paralyzed with shock. "Who-is-this?"

"He's… he's the Romano kid. He's the old man's grandson. You're not… you're not going to shoot him, are you?"

Dogrun heaved a sigh that chilled my blood. He was actually considering it.

"If you shoot me," I said, not quite knowing where the words came from, "it'll only make things worse."

There was a long silence.

"Come on," said Dogrun, waving the gun. "We're all going for a little ride."

I felt something wrenching my gut, and my legs were like rubber as we walked down the stairs. Dogrun was pointing his gun at me and made me march in front of the group. Gross and Snopengaard were struck dumb and walked quietly next to him. I was stunned with fear and unable to think clearly. All I knew was that something bad was about to happen, and I had no clue how to get out of my predicament.

Ironically, I was able to notice silly details on our way to the parking lot. How it had been recently paved, and what a big contrast that was with the Arcadia Train Station. I was surprised at how clean Snopengaard's car was. It smelled of lavender, and there was a sheen on everything, on the steering wheel and the dashboard. I could see no cups or wrappings or receipts or small papers, no trash at all, as if the car had just been rolled out of the shop.

As we drove off, I looked over my shoulder at the township building. They hadn't seen Sally, and I was glad she was out of danger. Then I turned back and fixed my eyes on Snopengaard. He was grabbing the steering wheel with both hands, his arms flexing at sharp angles, so that his face was almost pressed to the windshield. He was agitated and kept gesticulating as he drove, arguing with Dogrun, who rode shotgun. Gross sat next to me in the back seat, stiff and wide-eyed.

After a while, I looked out the window and noticed we had taken a dirt road.

Where the hell are we going?

I had to get my wits back. I began opening and closing my hands, feeling my fingers curl into fists, then extending them all the way. Once, and again, and again. Then I followed my breathing. I noticed it was shallow and agitated. I tried to take deeper, longer breaths and then made my hand extensions match my breathing. Slowly, I began to snap out of my trance of terror.

The gibberish between Snopengaard and Dogrun became intelligible, and I was able to follow what they were talking about.

"Once again, Dogrun, this is crazy. If you hurt the boy, it will be worse for us all. Just let him go. He's got nothing on us."

Dogrun seemed to consider, but after a moment, he sighed and shook his head.

"No loose ends. The stakes are too high for me. We do it my way."

It dawned on me that if I did nothing, I would die. *Maybe I could jump out of the moving car*, I thought. Since he had taken the dirt road, Snopengaard had reduced his speed. I figured I could roll out of the car onto the shrubbery without serious injury. But I hesitated nevertheless. Falling out of a moving car turned out to be scarier than I thought.

Eventually, I found the determination. I took a deep breath, counted to three, pulled the handle, and shoved the door with my shoulder.

It didn't budge.

"Don't even think of it," said Dogrun. "We're almost there."

Maybe they won't kill me, I thought. *Maybe they're just trying to scare me, to threaten me into silence.*

I took some comfort in the idea. I could play along with that. I would swear silence and pretend to be thankful for my life. I would even cry if that helped. I made my hands into fists again and focused on my breathing.

I shouldn't entertain that thought. It's just a form of avoidance. Dogrun will shoot. He will kill me. I have to do something about it.

The car stopped and Dogrun waved his gun at me, opening the door for me to step out. It was dark, but I knew exactly where we were. The rushing sound of the Whistana and the township safety tape were all I needed. We were at the site of the future bridge.

Dogrun heaved a sigh, shook his head, and said a few words to himself that I couldn't understand.

I had to buy some time.

"Before you do anything you might regret," I said, "I just want to remind you that I am the son of Margaret Grimshaw."

It was all I could think of. It was a stupid, meaningless threat. The name probably meant nothing to Dogrun. And even if it did, the information was probably to my disadvantage. However, the sound of my voice, words coming out of my mouth at that critical moment, had some unexpected effects.

Snopengaard, for one, froze. His jaw dropped as if he'd suddenly realized something. It had nothing to do with my mother, or with Grimshaw Realty. It was something else. My words seemed to remind him that I was a human being. One about to be executed. I hoped, for a moment, this would inspire him to take some action on my behalf. Anything. But he just stood there shaking like he might have a heart attack or something.

"And this," said Dogrun, "is supposed to mean something to me?"

"Yes," I said with unexpected confidence. "You don't know my mother. And you're lucky you don't. If I were you, I'd keep it that way."

Dogrun snickered, but again, my words seemed to have an effect, this time on Gross, who finally snapped out of his daze. He began to shake his head and mutter gibberish, pacing back and forth and grabbing his head.

"Don't make this difficult, kid," said Dogrun. "Take a step back. There. That's better."

The Whistana roared behind me. I was standing a few inches from the ledge about ten feet above the water.

Maybe I should jump, I thought, but the image of my skull cracking against a boulder gave me pause.

"What in the fucking world are we doing?"

It was Gross. He was freaking out. He began waving

his arms, walking in circles, weaving his way between the headlights and Dogrun and myself.

"This is madness! Put that fucking gun away. Have you lost your mind? We're all going to prison. This is not what I signed up for!"

He yelled that last sentence into Snopengaard's face, who whimpered and took a step back.

"Calm down, man. Get a grip," said Dogrun.

"Calm down? Calm down, you say? Are you mad? The only reason you're here is because Snopengaard is an idiot." He turned to Snopengaard. "How could you do this? You brought a money-laundering, gun-bearing gangster into a simple real estate deal. How stupid can you possibly be? You've ruined my life."

"Hey, man, take it easy," said Dogrun. "Calm down or I'll shoot you too."

Gross didn't seem to hear him. He was pacing again and grabbing his head, mumbling something about prison. And then Snopengaard spoke.

"Let me remind you… Samuel," he began in his sanctimonious tone.

That did it.

Gross completely lost it.

He charged against Snopengaard, and both men went to the ground, lifting a cloud of dust that swirled in the headlights. They wrestled in the dirt, and Gross managed to hold Snopengaard in a choke hold, pinning him to the ground. Snopengaard wriggled and managed to free himself, and soon both men were on their feet again, tugging at each other and swinging aimless, badly timed fists.

Dogrun slapped his thighs in frustration and walked over to the men.

"Come on now. Stop it, you two. Or I'll have to shoot all of you and then there will be no business. Hey! I said come on now."

Gross was still completely out of control. Upon hearing those words, he let go of Snopengaard, who gasped for air, and lunged at Dogrun, trying to shove him.

"Take it easy, man. Remember that I have the gun," said Dogrun.

"You piece of shit," yelled Gross and charged again. But Dogrun, who was stout and heavyset, barely budged. Gross then began flailing his arms, trying to connect a punch. This time Dogrun responded. He had lost his patience. Both men began to wrestle.

I thought I could make a dash for the bushes, but I would have to get past the men and the car, which was squeezed between the thick shrubbery, practically blocking the dirt road.

No, I realized, *that won't work.*

Then the gun went off.

There was a moment of stillness right after, the echoes of gunfire bouncing across the valley and ringing in our ears. Gross took a few clumsy steps and staggered toward me. There was blood all over him and terror in his eyes.

Dogrun shook his head and raised the gun toward us.

This was it.

I took a deep breath and grabbed Gross by the collar, lunging backward with all my strength, pulling us both over the cliff.

⌒

As my feet left the ground, I was suspended for a moment in a terrifying weightless state. My stomach rose in my body, and my muscles tensed in a panicked reflex, bracing for impact. Time slowed down, almost to a standstill, and my senses sharpened. I could see every star in the sky and hear each splash in the roaring river below us.

Then I saw a picture, an intricate map of my life. It resembled a curvy, winding labyrinth and reminded me of the vines in Nick's yard. There were more paths than I could count, twisting and turning, and crossing over one another in a massive entanglement of decisions, mistakes, triumphs, and blunders. I would always be the protagonist of this messy story, I realized, whether I liked it or not.

Being the hero, however, was quite a different matter. To be the hero in one's own story, one needed a deep sense of ownership, to be prepared to face the consequences of every choice with full and unflinching accountability. Like Achilles did when he chose his path, knowing he would die.

The sudden shock of the cold water forced the air out of my lungs in a muffled, bubbly scream.

CHAPTER 21

THE WHISTANA ROARED through the gorge, dragging us with it. I could feel the current change in strength and direction as it clashed against the stony banks and the boulders on its bed. At times, I was pulled forward at an even pace. At others, I was shoved, hitting against a rock or getting flushed through a gap.

In the darkness, I lost all sense of place and direction.

Then I heard a gurgling cry for help. It was coming from behind me, or so it seemed. When I heard it again, it was closer, right beside me. I reached out, grabbing, and eventually struck Gross's chest.

"Help," he managed to say, before gulping water and coughing beneath the surface. After several attempts, I was able to hold on to his jacket and pull him up as he gasped for air and flapped his arms.

I was able to get my bearings and realized we hadn't traveled that far. I knew the narrow section of the river was short, and I could still make out the steep banks on either side. Soon the course would widen and slow down, and I would be able to get some footing.

My feet dragged against pebbles, and I felt a brief jolt of

optimism. Then I was whisked up again, and I lost my hold on Gross. I tried to grab him, but there was nothing I could do against the current. My only choice was to let my body go limp and allow the river to wash me through the rapids.

Eventually, the roar died down and I felt solid ground beneath me. I crawled on stones and pebbles until I reached a sandy patch and let myself drop face down. I was exhausted, and I ached all over. All I wanted was to close my eyes and sleep.

And I almost did, but a little splash behind me put me on alert again. I heard the splash once more. It reminded me of the brown trout I had seen in the pool upstream. But it wasn't a trout. It was Gross, his face floating barely above the surface. I yanked his jacket and dragged him ashore, where he had a coughing fit, water gushing from his mouth and nose. The poor bastard was still bleeding from the bullet wound in his shoulder.

"Can you hear me?"

I shook him. He didn't respond.

"Hey! Can you hear me?"

He mumbled something and then nodded briefly.

I had to sit him up.

There was a large rock a few yards away, straight and tall enough for him to rest his back on. He was heavier than I imagined, or maybe I was too exhausted. I tugged him up, folding my arms around his chest from behind, until he was in place and I was confident he wouldn't slump over.

My eyes began to sting, and I rubbed them and wiped my face with my forearm. There was blood everywhere. I touched my face and noticed a huge gash across my forehead, dripping blood in my eyes, onto Gross and his stupid jacket and the pebbles along the riverbank.

I needed to lie down.

I'll rest here for just for a minute, I thought, *until I catch my breath.*

❧

When I awoke, the first glow of dawn was beginning to show. I could see the pale glimmer of the Whistana—its temper appeased as it stretched out over the wider river-bed—and the forest climbing upward on the opposite side of the valley. Upstream, the trees along the gorge were lit up in flashing lights, red and blue.

I was still trying to figure out what it all meant when I heard my name.

"Andy!" The call came from afar. *It was Sally.*

"Andy!" She was running toward me.

But from where?

"Andy? Oh my God, Andy."

She was frantic. She touched my face and stared in horror at my forehead. Then she ran her fingers through my hair, feeling every inch of my head, checking for injuries. She did the same with my torso, and I flinched when she touched my ribs.

"You look terrible. We need to get you to a medic."

I nodded. My face was completely covered in blood, caked and mixed with mud in some parts, still dripping in others.

"I need to hear you, Andy. Are you alright?"

"I'm fine. You should see the other guy," I said.

She laughed and cried and punched me in the shoulder.

"I was worried!" she said in tears and put her arms around me. She felt so warm. I wished we could melt together, disappear into a world in which only she and I existed.

"I love you," I said in her ear.

"I love you too, numb nuts," she said and gave me a little squeeze.

"But how did you find me?"

She didn't tell me right away. There were other—more urgent—things to do, like directing the paramedics to Gross and getting my bloody face looked at. They were worried I might have a concussion.

The police were busy too. As far as I could tell, they had apprehended Dogrun and Snopengaard, which was good. It meant the documents and plans were still safe in the township building, available for the investigation that would ensue.

In the days that followed, however, Sally told me more about that night, and I was able to reconstruct what had happened after we separated.

She was still crouching under the desk in the far corner when Dogrun waved his gun and ushered us out into the parking lot. While Snopengaard fidgeted with his keys and argued in stutters and half-sentences with Dogrun, Sally sneaked out of the building and crossed the street toward Nick's Honda and drove—lights out—around the corner and back to the main road, where she had a line of sight to the township building.

The four of us were still standing around Snopengaard's car, who was agitated as he spoke. I realized later he was trying to talk Dogrun out of doing something crazy. I don't think murder was ever part of his plan—he didn't have it in him—but he was clearly out of his depth and things had gotten out of hand.

Dogrun was getting impatient, and Gross and I were dazed and in shock, just standing there, waiting to be told what to do. Looking back, I realized I could have made a run at that moment. The side streets were dark, and I was in better shape than any of them. While they argued, I could have dashed across the main road and disappeared into the darkness.

Dogrun might have shot me in the back; that's true. But it was unlikely. Gunfire in the middle of a quiet town and a dead kid in the township building parking lot would be the end of their little enterprise.

Meanwhile, Sally waited around the corner.

When Snopengaard's car finally hit the road, it took a right toward Laurel Hill. That was all the information Sally needed. There was no exit to the highway down that road, so it wasn't hard for her to tell where we were heading. We were going either to the Collinsworth Estate or to Snopengaard's house.

Once the car was out of sight, she drove toward Redwood Road, keeping her distance. Then she called 911.

"What is your location? Where should we send the police units?"

"I'll tell you where exactly in a moment," said Sally, "but they're definitely heading to Laurel Hill."

"Miss, are you in pursuit of the vehicle right now?"

"I am," said Sally.

"You must stop immediately," said the operator. "Desist and stay out of harm's way. Do you understand? Let the police take over from here. Stop the vehicle."

"The hell I will," said Sally and drove on.

But by the time she reached the end of Redwood Road, she realized something was wrong. Snopengaard's car was nowhere to be seen. It had simply vanished. She could see the end of the road in her headlights, but there was nothing. To her right was the Collinsworth Estate and to her left, the short street that led to Snopengaard's house. There were no cars in the driveway either. No signs of any movement.

"Where did you go?" she muttered.

Then she remembered the map labeled *Subdivision Plat* we had seen in Snopengaard's office. On the map, the road to the bridge made a wide turn around the Collinsworth Estate, connecting to the back roads of Laurel Hill. The road hadn't been built yet—as far as we knew—but something told Sally it was worth a try.

She drove down every street and lane in Laurel Hill, circling around each cul-de-sac, shining her headlights on every curb, searching for any sign of access to a new road. She wondered whether she was just wasting her time, dreading what might happen to me if she was late. But just as she was about to give up, she saw an opening in the curb and the access to the dirt road.

She called 911 again.

"I know where they are," she told the operator and gave directions.

"Units are on their way," said the operator. "Stay where you are. Are you listening? Do not go any further. If you do, you might alert the perpetrators and interfere with law enforcement. I repeat. Stay where you are."

This time Sally obeyed. She waited by the car, wringing her hands and counting the seconds for the police to arrive. It would be daybreak soon, she realized, and hoped they wouldn't harm me until the police—or daylight—saved me.

Then the gun went off and echoed through the valley.

CHAPTER 22

NICK WAS DISCHARGED from the hospital a few days later. His infection had receded, and he was back on his cancer medication. He was in good spirits as well, a bit wobbly when he walked, but eager to get back to his home, his books, and his terraced yard.

"You look like you need a hospital more than I do," he joked when he saw me.

He was right. My face was swollen and bruised after being battered by the Whistana. On top of that, I had undergone plastic surgery to mend the gash, and thick black stitches formed a gruesome line across my forehead. They said all layers of skin and tissue had been slashed, right down to the skull. They also said I'd been lucky; I could have smashed my head right open. Instead, all I would get was a nasty scar, a line rising from my right eyebrow, curving all the way to my temple.

Sally liked it. She said I looked "badass."

It was sunny and dry when we brought Nick home. Throughout his stay at the hospital, my father and I had carefully avoided the subject of him moving, in part because we didn't want to upset him, in part because it was a good excuse to avoid a difficult conversation.

It was Nick who brought up the subject. He had made up his mind.

"It's time for me to move," he said, slapping his thighs to stress his resolution. "It only makes sense… I'll be better off in Bradwick, spending more time with books and less time fighting wineberries and English ivy. Maybe I'll write a memoir."

We were all silent for a moment, sitting on the deck chairs, looking out at the valley in the afternoon sun. This was the view Nick adored, the one he had enjoyed for decades, the one that, even during the dark times he'd had to face, had been there as a lifeline, a perspective, a reminder of how vast the world was.

It broke my heart. Maybe things would've turned out differently if—I don't know—I had worked harder, or confronted Snopengaard earlier.

Nick was smiling. He seemed to notice what I was thinking.

"I knew this was coming, Andy," he tried to reassure me. "I knew it all along. It's not such a catastrophe; it's just life. It has its cycles, its stages. There's a time and place for everything. You see, I would have moved out anyway. After Mimi left us, my days in this house were numbered. Besides, moving will be good for me. You'll see."

We agreed we would wait until the end of summer to list the house. All the drama with Courtyard Therapeutics was still up in the air, and Arcadia was in the news for all the wrong reasons. It would take time to find a buyer, and what seemed best to us all was that I should stay with Nick for a few months until school started in September. My father would go back to work and start scouting for a new place in Bradwick, something with a small yard for Nick to work on.

Back in Chicago, my mother had finally picked someone else to represent Grimshaw at the conference. She explained to the board that I was recovering from a car accident and that our plans were on hold for the time being. She was very upset. She told me she was disappointed, but I had a feeling she really felt betrayed. The door was closing for me at Grimshaw, if it hadn't already.

I didn't care anymore. I had realized, as I plunged into the Whistana, that I would not be a character in her story, and I was willing to face the consequences of that decision, whatever they were. Besides, I was looking forward to the remainder of my stay in Arcadia. I would spend time with Sally before she returned to Harrisburg, and in the evenings, I would discuss the Greek heroes with Nick. It was exactly the kind of summer I needed.

Nick insisted we change the tractor parts and get the yard mowed. He couldn't bear the sight of it, he said. He also claimed it was important, that he owed it to the house and to Mimi. He said I should bear witness to the change before the summer was over, that I should see the yard as it had been all those years ago.

"I want to leave this house in the best shape I can, Andy," he said.

And with that, he began to snap orders.

First, he told me to carry the tractor parts to the shed. On my second trip, I walked beside him, making sure he kept his balance and was shielded from the sun.

He grunted as he stooped, and once in position, he got to work. He would call out for a tool and I would hand it to him, returning the one he no longer needed to the box. I got most of his instructions wrong. He would say things like "half-inch socket" or "battery terminal puller" and, realizing I had no idea what tool he meant, would point at it with his finger.

"No. Not that one. *That* one," he would say every now and then.

Sally thought this was hilarious and couldn't stop laughing.

The torque wrench clicked, and the faulty gas pump came loose. Nick also changed the battery, spark plugs, and filters, and soon the ignition whined and the engine putted, coughing spasmodically at first and letting out billows of black smoke before it began to run smoothly.

At Nick's signal, I hopped on and drove the tractor out of the shed and onto the tall green grass.

"So, I just go?" I asked.

"No! If you don't engage the blades, you'll just be riding around. Here"—he pointed to a lever on the right side of the seat—"this will adjust the height of the blade deck. The grass is very tall, so just in case, let's set it on the highest notch. Here."

The deck clanked as it fit into position.

"Now all that's left is to engage the blades." He pointed to a switch beside the steering wheel. "Go slowly and try to make straight lines."

He clicked his tongue and patted the back of the tractor as if it were a horse. Sally hurried and climbed up to sit behind me, squeezing her arms around my waist.

"Let's go, cowboy," she said.

Back and forth we went, and with each strip of mowed grass, my lines became straighter and the overlaps between them tighter. The blades crunched the mesh of leaves and stems beneath us, sending out a compact burst of lush debris through the shoot and leaving behind a smooth carpet of bright green.

It took us no more than half an hour to mow the entire yard—front and back—and I felt triumphant as I looked around. The yard was open once again, the terraces were visible, the stone steps stood proud and ensured safe passage between one level and the next, and right at the very center of it all, the firepit stood like an altar for some ancient god, ready to take offerings of fat and bones.

It was hard to believe. In mere minutes, the long grass, the cause of so much trouble, was finally tamed and put in its place. It was only grass. And that's what it had been all along.

"Well," said Nick, looking in the direction of Snopengaard's house, "we are now in compliance with township ordinances." He wasn't gloating, and there was nothing condescending in his attitude. Quite the contrary, there seemed to be sadness in his voice and I got the impression he felt sorry for Snopengaard.

Things weren't looking good for our neighbor.

Right after the incident, Sally had made contact with her friends in Harrisburg who, in turn, involved the office of the district attorney. The very next day, investigators raided the township building, seizing documents and confiscating computers for forensic analysis. Snopengaard's office was sealed off with police tape as the formal investigation took place.

That same night, a statement was released by the

township. It said the administration was being investigated for criminal misconduct and confirmed that Karl Snopengaard had been removed from his position. The interim township manager would be Bernard Higgins, Sally's father.

It was the talk in town. All of a sudden, everyone in Arcadia swore they had been suspicious about Snopengaard all along. One could tell, they all agreed, he had the look of someone who was up to something. I found it interesting that people no longer referred to him as "Chuck" or "Mr. Snopengaard" and instead called him plainly "Snopengaard" as if he had been degraded in some way.

Following his interrogation, Snopengaard had been released on bail and remained holed up in his house, waiting for the case to go to trial. He faced multiple charges, including abuse of public office, falsification of records, real estate fraud, and harassment.

As for Samuel Gross, he had barely survived that fateful night. He was in shock and seriously wounded when I pulled him into the Whistana. I'd saved him from Dogrun's gun alright, but I'd put him in a different sort of danger altogether, unable as he was to keep afloat and completely disoriented. He swallowed a whole lot of water and must have taken a bad beating against the rocks.

He was fired from Courtyard Therapeutics—that almost goes without saying—and faced multiple charges for fraud. However, in a curious turn of events, he managed to strike a plea bargain in exchange for testifying against Dogrun. Dogrun, as it turned out, was a person of interest to the FBI.

It must have been Thursday. Or maybe Friday. My father had returned to Bradwick, and Nick was sleeping. He would take naps during the day and was usually asleep during most of the afternoon. He was still weak, but I suspected there was more to his naps than that. He had found some sort of peace. One could see it in his face. He would breathe deeper and chuckle more often, sometimes to himself. I saw him smile at the horizon one morning as he gazed at the valley from the deck. It wasn't the heavy smile I had seen when I arrived in Arcadia; now there was something like hope in it. I suppose he was at peace with what he was leaving behind and maybe even looking forward to something new.

I felt quite relaxed as well, as if I was enjoying a well-deserved vacation. There was no rush anymore. I had forfeited my internship and rid myself of all the pressures that came with it. Mother was still mad—and she would be for a while—but I knew the whole thing would eventually blow over.

I didn't have much to do, and I was savoring every moment of my idleness. That day, for example, I spent most of the afternoon on the deck, watching the clouds go by and the trees sway in the breeze. A groundhog had been trotting up and down the yard, and I watched it as it went about its business. It had probably lived there all along, the entrance to its burrow covered in thick vegetation. Now that the grass was mowed, it seemed happy enough to waddle and scamper in the open, and I was happy to watch it and let the hours go by.

Sally, on the other hand, was quite busy. The township staff members were still in shock after the events, trying to work as best they could in the midst of an investigation. They were also dealing with a change in management, helping Mr. Higgins get up to speed with the township agenda, its procedures, and its finances. Sally worked long hours beside her father. She knew all the ins and outs, not only of Arcadia but of Harrisburg too. And on the rare occasions when she didn't know something, she knew exactly whom to call and what strings to pull. Never had a township manager taken office with such an expert adviser as Sally was.

As the shadows stretched out and the valley began to glow in orange light, I became bored and decided to test my cookout skills. I had seen Nick light the fire and grill that delicious chicken, and I was confident I could do it as well. Besides, something told me a cookout under the stars was warranted. We had disbanded a criminal organization, saved the town from fraud and—on a smaller scale—prevailed over the vines and recovered Nick's precious yard. It was necessary to mark the occasion, to burn offerings to the gods and commemorate that special moment.

I carried the cooking grate and the skillet to the firepit and made several trips back and forth to the house, collecting utensils, ingredients, and condiments. Then I stacked a decent pile of firewood on the side of the pit and arranged three chairs around it, forming a semicircle.

It was harder than I thought. The kindling would light easily and blaze for a few moments, only to go out and leave nothing but traces of smoke. It took me a few of these failed attempts before I got a real fire going, and I watched with satisfaction as the flames began to lick the logs and make them crackle.

Nick joined me a moment later, summoned—it seemed—by the smell of smoke. He nodded when he saw the charring logs and took a seat, staring at times at the flames, other times at the sky and the stars that were beginning to show.

Once the logs were glowing red, I gave them a few taps—as I'd seen Nick do—and pushed the embers under the grate. Nick nodded again. I placed the chicken over the glowing bed and the chopped veggies in the skillet.

"So, this is where the party's at," we heard Sally say, as she stepped into the circle of light. She kissed me on the lips and ruffled my hair. "How's my badass?"

"Your badass has learned a thing or two," said Nick, signaling the chicken.

"Well, look at you," said Sally, and then she turned toward Nick. "Isn't he great?"

I pretended not to hear and stirred the veggies and checked on the chicken, wondering if it was time to turn the pieces over. I wasn't sure. I shot a quick glance at Nick, and he shook his head. I waited.

When we had eaten, Nick cleared his throat and asked us about that night.

"I've heard bits and pieces of the story," he said, "but I want to hear the whole thing in detail."

I told him about my walk down the Whistana that morning, about the discovery of the bridge site, and then about breaking into the township building and Snopengaard's office. Sally told her part of the story as well, how she drove around with the lights out until she had a line of sight to the parking lot, how she found the dirt road in Laurel Hill. That kind of stuff.

When we came to the episode of the gunshot, a strange feeling came over me, a buzz, as if something important was happening. I focused on my memories, trying to recall the details. I remembered seeing Gross freak out, struggle with Dogrun, and then turn toward me with blood all over his white shirt. I remember thinking Dogrun would finish him off and then shoot me as well. Gross and I, ironically, were on the same side in that moment. We were both about to be executed. That was when I pulled his jacket and lunged backward.

I told Nick and Sally about my strange experience as I was falling, how time had slowed down and I had a very clear understanding of what it meant to be the hero in one's own story.

Nick's eyes grew wide, and he encouraged me to go on. I told him what I had thought, that being the hero in one's own story was all about a sense of ownership of our path in life. A commitment to unflinching accountability, the unwavering acceptance of responsibility for one's actions. I told him it was just like with Achilles, who had chosen his path knowing he would die.

Nick was speechless and kept smacking his lips and looking up at the stars.

"That's one hell of a story," he said at last. He was shaking his head and smiling. "Look at you… Look at you… Quite the Achilles you turned out to be, walking down the heroic path, just like the heroes of our mythical past."

"Well," I said, feeling put on the spot, "I'm not so sure about that."

You're my hero, mouthed Sally and batted her eyelashes. We both laughed.

"Well, that's all very nice," I said. "I know I'm on my own path and all that. And I know I don't want to be a character in someone else's story. But I still have no idea what to do. I mean, what path am I on? What am I supposed to do? I still don't know, to put it in your words, what my story will be about."

"And that's how it should be," said Nick. "At least for now." He nodded as he spoke.

"What do you mean?"

"What I mean is that, by the looks of it, you've just gone through your second act. You've crossed the threshold of initiation. You've had your Apotheosis"—he looked at my scar and gestured with his chin—"but the whole thing still needs to come together."

He scratched his beard and was lost in thought for a while.

"So, what does Mr. Hero Badass need to do for… things to come together?" asked Sally.

"Well," said Nick, the flames dancing on his face. "The third act, the last stage of the hero's journey, is called the 'Return.' That's what you must face now."

"That makes no sense at all, Nick. I've just made up my mind to spend the rest of the summer right here with you in Arcadia. I'm not returning anytime soon."

Nick chuckled and made a funny face.

"Maybe I should tell you about Odysseus."

CHAPTER 23

THE AIR HAD begun to turn as it did in the evenings. Once the sun had gone down and the warmth of the day had drained from the hillsides, the heat stored in the valley rose. It felt like a warm breeze and carried the smell of water. But after an hour or so of dark, as the hills lost their warmth faster than the Whistana Basin, came a reversal, a downslope breeze of cool air pooling by the river like mist returning from where it had come.

I threw in another log to keep the fire going, and Sally curled up beside me and covered her arms with a blanket I had brought for her.

"Let's hear it, Nick," she said. "Tell us about Odysseus."

"It will be a pleasure," he said. "I mentioned Odysseus when I told you the story of Achilles, but he has his own story—many of them, in fact."

Nick paused for a moment. Then he looked at us and raised his finger.

"And just as I did with many of these stories, I will tell you only a summary, just enough to illustrate my point."

Sally and I looked at each other, and we both nodded.

"Odysseus was born in Ithaca, a small island in the Ionian Sea. He was a smart young boy and a fast learner and became proficient at anything he set out to learn. He was witty and had a way with words and always seemed to come out on top in any situation.

"He married Penelope, a beautiful princess of Sparta, and had a son called Telemachus. But when Telemachus was still a baby, the Trojan War broke out and Odysseus was summoned to join the campaign. During the war, he played a crucial role. It was him, in fact, who devised the famous trick of the Trojan Horse, which finally decided the war's outcome.

"But the story of Odysseus—as told by Homer in *The Odyssey*—takes place after the war, when he and his men sailed back to Ithaca. It's a story about *nostos*, about the return or homecoming.

"His voyage took ten years and was riddled with misfortune. He shipwrecked several times and was often within an inch of his life, fighting strange enemies and escaping all kinds of danger. The collection of his adventures at sea is known as 'The Great Wanderings.'

"Let see." He stared into the fire, thinking. "He met the Lotus-eaters who tempted his men with forgetfulness. He blinded the cyclops Polyphemus and then barely escaped the giant Laestrygonians." Nick was counting with his fingers. "He rescued his men from the sorceress Circe and spent a year with her on her island. He even went to the underworld to visit the spirits of the dead, which is a great story. What else? After that he heard the song of the sirens—and survived to tell that tale—and managed to get through the legendary straight between Scylla and Charybdis. Eventually, shipwrecked and barely alive, alone after all his men were dead, he became the prisoner of the goddess Calypso, who wanted him for a husband. Seven years he stayed on her island."

"That's a long list," said Sally. "It looks like getting back home was pretty hard."

"That's right, young lady. That's right. And that's why, by the way, we still call a long and difficult journey an 'odyssey.'"

He made a funny face and Sally giggled.

"But the point is, my dears, that throughout his many adventures and misfortunes, Odysseus never lost sight of his goal: to return to Ithaca. All along, as he dealt with seemingly insurmountable obstacles, he always longed for his home. His resolve never wavered. And the long list of troubles he faced only stresses the importance of his return."

The fire died out and began to smoke. It stung our eyes and made us cough, and I hurried to add another log, which lit up at once and cleared the fumes.

"Sorry," I said. "I got distracted."

"So, how did he get home?" asked Sally.

"Well… In the end, and with some help from the gods—Athena above all—the noble Phaeacians would help Odysseus get back to Ithaca. They put him on a fine ship and carried him back home."

I pictured myself boarding the plane to O'Hare and thought of Mother's house in Chicago and my apartment at Lindenfield. They didn't seem like home to me, not at that moment at least. They seemed, in fact, remote and strange, part of another life that I had no intention of returning to. I mean, I would, at the end of the summer, just long enough to get my degree and move on. *Move on where? Where was home, anyway? And what was it? What did one return to?*

"Pay attention." Sally elbowed me. "So, that's where the story ends?" she asked Nick.

"Oh no," said Nick. "There's quite a bit more to it."

"But wasn't he back in Ithaca?" I asked. "Doesn't that make his return complete?"

"No." Nick shook his head. "For his return to be complete, Odysseus still needed to reconnect with his life as it was before he left. He needed to reinstate himself in his former roles, as husband, father, and king. And that wouldn't be easy, given the state of affairs in Ithaca."

"What happened in Ithaca?" Sally asked.

"His long absence had created many problems. You see, once the war had ended and the heroes of other kingdoms had returned to their homes, Odysseus was absent—he disappeared, in fact, for another ten years. As you can imagine, everyone believed he was dead. There was no way he was still alive. This made Penelope a widow and, as such, eligible for marriage."

"And that was a bad thing?" Sally asked, shrugging.

"Yes. Penelope was the lady of the house and retained some authority in Ithaca, especially over Odysseus's estate. With Odysseus dead, she was expected to choose a consort, who would become the regent of Ithaca and take possession of everything Odysseus owned.

"Naturally, this was very tempting, so over the course of a few years, more than a hundred arrogant noblemen became Penelope's suitors. They quite literally invaded Odysseus's palace and feasted every day on his cattle and drank the wine from his cellars while they waited for Penelope to choose one of them as a husband.

"Day after day, they consumed Odysseus's goods and wealth, they mocked the absent king, and they harassed Penelope, pressing her to make up her mind. This went on for years, and the more she stalled, the more the tension escalated, affecting every aspect of the kingdom to the point that even the people of Ithaca began to lose sympathy for their queen. She was very much alone in her plight, and she and her son were in mortal danger."

"But Odysseus was already back," said Sally. "Wouldn't that settle the issue?"

"Things, unfortunately, had escalated to a point where that was impossible. If Odysseus showed himself at his palace, the suitors would kill him immediately. They were, in fact, already planning to kill Telemachus."

"So, what happened? What did he do?" I asked.

"Well," said Nick, "just as he had during the war and all along his troubled journey, Odysseus would have to use his clever mind to come up with a strategy. He first disguised himself as a beggar and stayed at the house of his old swineherd, a short distance from the palace.

"He only revealed his identity to his son Telemachus, who was first in disbelief and denial. I don't think it was easy for the boy, you know? I mean, even as he started to realize the man in front of him was indeed Odysseus, there were mixed feelings toward a father who'd been absent all his life."

I thought of my own father. *Hadn't he, in his own way, struggled to reconnect with me? What kind of odyssey had he been on? I would have to ask him some day…* I shook off the thought. Nick was still talking.

"… was the first step in restoring Odysseus in his old roles."

"But what about the suitors?" asked Sally. "How did he deal with those?"

"Ha," said Nick. "Remember, Odysseus was very clever. First, he returned to his own palace, still in disguise, looking like a poor old beggar. This way, he was able to wander his own halls incognito, checking out the suitors, taking stock of their weapons, and identifying loyal versus disloyal servants. He did a little bit of espionage, so to speak.

"He even got to speak to Penelope, who told him of her sorrows and about the many tricks she'd used to delay the suitors, always hoping for her husband to return. This was very important for Odysseus. You see, he needed to know where things stood between them and how she would react upon seeing him again. Just imagine, the lost husband appearing out of the blue after twenty years, all alone after losing all his men.

"The next day, under unbearable pressure and somewhat encouraged by her conversation with the mysterious beggar, Penelope made her way to the main hall, carrying with her the bow and quiver that had belonged to her husband. In front of the suitors, she announced she would marry the man who was able to string Odysseus's great bow and shoot an arrow through twelve ax-heads. All the suitors tried, but none of them succeeded. Then Odysseus, still disguised as a beggar, asked for his turn."

"Let me guess," said Sally. "He was able to do it, right?"

"Right. Odysseus strung the bow with ease and completed the challenge. All were astonished, and before they had any time to react, Odysseus aimed his next arrow at the leader of the suitors, who was still holding a gold cup of wine, and struck him in the throat. With the help of Telemachus and a few loyal servants, Odysseus killed every single one of the suitors in a brutal reckoning until the halls of the palace were covered in blood."

"How gruesome," said Sally, making a face of disgust.

"The massacre is symbolic," said Nick. "It represents the cleansing of the rot that had festered in his absence. It's a dramatic reassertion of moral order."

"And what about Penelope?" asked Sally.

"Well, as you can imagine, she was skeptical. Was it really him? After all those years? Or was she being tricked by yet another evil suitor? But here's the thing, Penelope was just as clever as her husband and always had some cunning plan. What do you think she did?"

"Well," said Sally, "if I were her, I would test him. I would ask him questions only he would know the answers to." She elbowed me again and winked.

Nick laughed and slapped his thighs.

"What a Penelope you would have turned out to be, young Sally."

"And so, what then? They lived happily ever after?" I asked.

Nick chuckled. "I don't think the Greeks were familiar with the concept of a happy ending, but I suppose you could say something like that. At least at the end of *The Odyssey*, Odysseus was reunited with his wife and his son, and order was restored in Ithaca."

He remained silent for a while and we all looked around, each with our own thoughts. In the distance, I could see the faint glow of Harrisburg, like a misty haze rising from the ground. The valley was dark, and it occurred to me that Nick's house was like a small island of light in the vast night. This house was his place in the world. If he were to return from some faraway journey, he would be returning here, no doubt. He had built a history here, a lifetime, an identity. I, on the other hand, was just getting started with my life. *Where was home for me? It probably didn't even exist. At least not yet.*

Sally cuddled against me.

"So, tell me," said Nick, looking at us. "What do you make of this story?"

"It's about the return of Odysseus," I said with confidence. "On the surface, he's returning to his homeland in Ithaca, but I suspect there's more to his… What did you call it? *Nostis?*"

"*Nostos.* Yes. Very good. *Nostos* is a common theme in Greek literature. You see, back then, going on a voyage was very dangerous. One left behind the safety of home and community, only to face the forces of nature and all sorts of enemies. So, you can see why returning home safely was such a big deal to them."

"But nowadays things are different," said Sally. "Why would this return be important to us? Why can't the hero just stay… wherever he is?" She put her arms around me and covered herself with the blanket.

"Ah…" said Nick, eyes shining. "That's because the Greeks also used this word to convey a different type of return."

"What do you mean?" asked Sally almost in a whisper.

"I mean a return that's psychological in nature. A return that's about coming full circle. You see, as the hero returns to the ordinary world—the one left behind in the first act—all the experiences of the quest are actualized. In a way, it all comes together, and the hero is finally able to integrate those experiences into the conscious mind."

"But if the return is psychological, why must heroes

sail back to their homeland?" asked Sally and glanced my way. "Why do they have to travel back home?"

"Very clever, young Sally!" said Nick. "You're right, the psychological nature of the return implies that it isn't necessarily about returning physically to the homeland—or to any place in particular, for that matter. Remember that even when Odysseus arrived on the shores of Ithaca, his return wasn't complete. He still needed to step back into his old roles for that to happen.

"You see, by reconnecting with the old familiar world, heroes are finally able to take stock of how much they've changed. They are able to realize important things about themselves and begin to understand their place in the world." He gave me a meaningful look. "They may even figure out what their story is all about."

I sighed and shook my head. I had no intention of reconnecting with Grimshaw or with any of the roles my mother had set up for me. I knew I had changed. My experiences in Arcadia had transformed me in many ways, and I didn't need any *nostos* or "coming full circle" to know that.

Nick seemed to read my mind. He had that cheeky smile on his face.

"I'm afraid you must," he said. "One way or another, you need to reconnect with the world you left behind. You must come full circle. You've had your great adventure. Now you must finish what you started."

CHAPTER 24

THE DAYS THAT followed were long, and I spent most of my time waiting for Sally to return from work. It was ironic. I had been very much looking forward to a time of idle relaxation and felt disappointed when all I got was the boredom that comes with waiting. Boredom, and a vague, uneasy feeling, like a door left ajar or a crooked picture frame.

Something was bugging me.

Odysseus.

The return.

The idea of returning to my life as it was before—before my trip to Arcadia, that is—made me recoil. Nick had insisted it was important. So important, in fact, that the hero's journey wasn't complete until it happened. But I resisted the entire premise. I had changed. I had a new perspective on myself and my path in life. *What need was there to return—or "reconnect" as Nick said—with the old world, with all its complicated relationships and dynamics?*

To kill time, I took long walks around the Collinsworth Estate and up and down the Whistana, following the gorge downstream all the way to the muddy banks and even beyond to the point where the river flowed again through a thick forest.

For some reason, I thought about Jason a lot, about what he wanted at the start of his journey—to become king and acquire what was his by birthright—and about how his path, even without him realizing it, would take him on a quest to find what he really needed.

What had I wanted at the start of my journey?

I suppose I'd wanted to get on with my career at Grimshaw and eventually take over the company from my mother. My quest, however, had taken me down a strange path and had led me to an unlikely situation. *But had it taken me, just as it did with Jason, to what I really needed? And what had I needed in the first place?*

Maybe, as Nick had said when we discussed the second act, I needed to reconfigure my relationship with my parents. *Yes, that made sense.* And I was confident, besides, that a lot had changed in that respect. I suppose I also needed to take the reins of my own life, to break away from my mother's grasp and make my story my own.

What I still couldn't figure out was what my story would be about, and to my dismay, Nick had insisted the answer could only be found in the metaphorical "Return," in the world I had left behind in Chicago.

Almost two weeks went by, and with each passing day, my body and my mind became more comfortable with my slow routine. My skin tanned from my long walks, and I came to enjoy the hot afternoons in the open fields as much as I enjoyed the cool breeze down by the Whistana. The scar on my forehead waned, and the clutter in my mind subsided. I suppose I became less resistant, more open about my future. Even my thoughts about the return lost some of their jagged edges, and I found myself wondering about Lindenfield and my home in Chicago.

One afternoon, after a particularly hot midday, it began to pour. It was one of those summer storms they call "single-cells," when the moist air from the ground rises too fast and then comes down in buckets.

Forced inside, and having nothing more interesting to do, I sat at my computer and found myself accessing the Grimshaw database. It was one of those thoughtless actions, I guess. I grimaced at the long procession of folders, the ones that had been marked as "mandatory reading" by my mother. It was so ironic all of a sudden. What my mother didn't seem to realize was just how much of their content I already knew by heart. It was as if she didn't trust me or my capabilities. The feeling was bitter.

I sighed and shook my head and was about to log out of the database and move on when I saw that mysterious folder again, the one at the bottom left of my screen.

Others it was titled. I remembered the file I had worked on: *Location Checklist and Criteria for Location Attractiveness*. It established a grading system to determine whether a town or locality held any promising return on investment. It was a faulty process, and I had fixed it, improved it. I had classified the criteria, separating variables that were given from those that could be affected by investment, policy, and infrastructure. With this new approach, Arcadia's numbers had improved significantly.

And then an idea struck me, and I began working on it.

I knew Arcadia had huge potential. I had discussed my thoughts with Higgins the day Sally and I had ice cream at his shop. He and Sally had seen this potential as well. Snopengaard, I realized, had also seen it in his own twisted way.

I reformulated the analysis of Arcadia, factoring in a new set of assumptions. *What if a bridge were built, connecting Laurel Hill directly to the highway, shortening the commute time to Harrisburg? What if a high-end residential neighborhood was established in the former Collinsworth Estate? What if a company like Courtyard Therapeutics were to refurbish one of the old factories, deal with land remediation and repurpose it as a research facility?*

I typed feverishly.

When I factored in Snopengaard's plan, the numbers were astounding. With some well-planned infrastructure, Laurel Hill —and Arcadia itself— could become a high-return investment. But Snopengaard had gone about the whole thing in the wrong way, using secrecy and intimidation. He had associated himself with criminals and had broken the law. Furthermore, his actions had been driven by the wrong reasons. "This town owes me enough already," I'd heard him say to Gross when Sally and I were hiding behind the filing cabinet.

Then it occurred to me that there might be a better way.

I kept on typing, imagining scenarios of my own. *What if the Township of Arcadia worked on land remediation and building restoration and transformed the strip of old factories into a research hub? Maybe there could be some sort of tax incentive.*

My hands were shaking as I worked. I wrote down all

my thoughts and adjusted them as new ideas came barging
into my mind.

I was formulating a plan.
And it was a good one.
I had to talk to Sally.
I had to talk to Collinsworth.
I had to talk to Mr. Higgins.
It was urgent.

Maybe, I realized, *I might even have to talk to my
mother…*

Arcadia Capital was signed into existence on a Thursday
morning in August, under the heavy stillness of midsum-
mer. The company was registered in a quiet corner of the
Midport County Courthouse, and three of us signed the
forms, spelling our names with slow, deliberate movements
to mark the solemnity of the moment.

Gregory Pierpoint Collinsworth contributed the rolling hills of his undeveloped land—which we all knew as
the Collinsworth Estate—where most of the new Laurel
Hill community would be located. At his request, and in a
slight departure from the original plans, we had agreed to
keep the old manor—the "proper chateaux," as Nick had
called it—and use it as a clubhouse.

Sarah—Sally—Higgins contributed her knowledge of
grants and zoning and the politics of funding streams. She
had been critical in restoring conversations with Courtyard
Therapeutics and steering them back to their original plan
of using the old cork factory as a research facility. She also
got the paperwork and all the proper authorizations for the
new road to the highway and the bridge over the Whistana

Gorge and negotiated the upgrade of the power grid and waterworks for the new neighborhood. Once Arcadia Capital took off, she would advise on public administration matters and manage government and regulatory affairs.

And I—Andrew Romano—contributed my knowledge of commercial real estate, which my mother had drilled into me for years. My job would be to work on the execution of the project and its commercialization. My plan was to return to Lindenfield to obtain my degree and then move back to Harrisburg where Sally and I would run Arcadia Capital together.

But in that simple ceremony, under the vaulted ceiling of the county courthouse, something else came into existence. Arcadia Capital was meant to be much more than a real estate development company. The spirit of what we were doing went beyond profits. It was an aspiration to build something elevated and good, something that would contribute to the heritage and the communities of small towns throughout the country.

We created, for example, a long-term fund out of a capital reserve fed by a percentage of annual profits, which would be directed toward land remediation of the industrial strip on the other end of town. Any rescued facility would be leased and the proceedings would go toward township infrastructure.

Mr. Higgins—and The Three Elders—had agreed to a program of tax breaks for companies interested in establishing research facilities and precision manufacturing plants. There were ongoing conversations with Harrisburg to clear state tax incentives and funding as well. Some companies had already shown interest, and negotiations were popping up here and there.

There was one sticking point, which I managed to rein in before we formally registered the company: Snopengaard's house. His property was critical to the project, and because it was closer to the Collinsworth Estate than Nick's, both homes needed to become part of the new Laurel Hill.

I agonized over this for days and finally decided to simply walk over to Snopengaard's home and knock on the door.

He wouldn't talk to me.

I thought he was bitter and angry at me, maybe because I had ruined his ambitions and his career. But it turned out he was terrified of me as if I were some apparition from the netherworld, coming to claim compensation for my—almost—murder.

Irina, his wife, was the one who finally opened the door. Snopengaard moved nervously in the background, like a curious—albeit jumpy—squirrel. Irina turned out to be very smart, and despite Snopengaard's whimpering protests, she agreed to sell the house. I had offered a very generous sum, more than the Snopengaards would ever get if they sold it to anyone else, but less than what Karl had hoped to win with his devious and ill-fated plan. I guess Irina knew their options were limited and they would have to move far away from Arcadia anyway.

That was, in short, how we formed Arcadia Capital, part real estate development firm, part strategic recovery of forgotten towns. If we succeeded, Arcadia would become a beacon, a shining example of how other towns could also realize their full potential. Nick would say that those towns would become heroes in their own stories.

I spoke to my mother in the early phases of our development of Arcadia Capital. I initially explained my thought process to her and she listened. I wasn't nervous. I had little or nothing to lose at that point. Besides, my whole adventure in Arcadia had turned me into a different person. It had made me assertive and had given me a renewed sense of assurance, making me immune to her old routine of threats and pressure.

She must have perceived something had changed in me. She probably was also aware, once it was clear I wanted no part in Grimshaw and was not calling to apologize, that she had lost much of the leverage she had over me. She was no fool. And so, she listened.

But she was skeptical, nonetheless. She didn't trust Collinsworth.

"He's an old Wall Street shark. You better keep your eyes open."

Before signing Arcadia Capital into existence, I gave her another call. It was very civilized. I told her we could use additional financial strength and the negotiating power of a larger conglomerate and proposed to integrate Arcadia Capital into the Grimshaw holding. This move would also be beneficial to Grimshaw, as it would add a new and independent income stream to its business structure.

"There are a couple of conditions, that is, if we were to move forward along these lines," I said. "Arcadia Capital would have to be an autonomous division of Grimshaw and respond to the board directly."

There was a long silence.

But it was a different kind of silence.

She wasn't using it to build tension or to calculate her next move. I believe she was *feeling* something.

"That's a good proposal, Andy," she said. There was something strange in her voice, and she had to clear her throat. "But it doesn't fit Grimshaw's strategic priorities. I can't allocate capital to something like this, and I'm not willing to diversify our core business."

"I understand," I said. It was fine. We had enough capital to go ahead without her, and Courtyard Therapeutics gave us enough momentum to get off the ground.

It's probably better this way, I thought.

"Andy," she said after a while, "I hope you… I hope you understand I've always wanted what's best for you. Sometimes… I guess, sometimes I can be a bit harsh. Anyway, what I want to say is that I…"

I held my breath.

"That I'm impressed," she said finally.

That summer came to an official end in late August when I returned to Lindenfield to complete my senior year. Nick, as we had agreed, would move to Bradwick, to a nice brick twin with a little yard, where he could grow tomatoes and cucumbers. I would drive him to Bradwick in his Honda, where he would stay with my father until everything was settled and he could move to his new home.

It was especially hot that day, and the cicadas hummed with urgency. I sat on the front porch and waited while Nick spent time inside the house by himself. He said he needed to make sure he was not forgetting anything, but he was probably saying his goodbyes.

When he finally walked out the front door, he nodded

briefly and we headed toward the car. He was carrying a book in his hand, which he handed to me as he patted my shoulder. The book was *Heroikos*, the same little green volume he had kept on his shelf for so many years.

"A little memento," he said, and his face broke into a smile that said a thousand words.

"So, this is it. This is 'officially' it, I mean. My return. My *nostos*," I said.

"You've already had your *nostos*, dear Andy," said Nick, putting his hand on my shoulder.

"I know," I said, "but you know what I mean. Now I am actually returning to Chicago, at least for now."

Nick sighed and made an almost imperceptible nod. He was looking around, taking in the view for the last time.

"Your return. My departure," he said.

I hadn't realized that. I had been focused on what the stages of the hero's journey meant in my own story. But he was right, of course. He was leaving his home behind, going off to some new and unknown part of his personal story.

"It's kind of poetic, if you think about it," he continued, still looking vaguely in direction of the Collinsworth Estate.

"What do you mean?"

I also looked around at the rolling green hills against the deep blue sky. I thought about heroes departing, saying farewell to their loved ones as they embarked on their quests. They would all return some day, only they would no longer be the same person who left. They would be transformed.

"So?" I insisted.

"Well, the hero's departure means leaving behind the

ordinary world, what's known and familiar. *Nostos* is a metaphorical return to the starting point, where the hero is once again ready to go on another quest. And just like you and me, heroes are always returning and always departing. It's like a circle."

From where we stood, I could see a portion of the backyard and the blooming azaleas that flanked the stone steps. I took a deep breath through my nose, allowing the warm, perfumed air to fill my lungs, and immediately remembered that day from my childhood. I was wearing those shiny blue shoes I had seen on TV.

At Nick's signal, I had dashed up the terraces, pumping my legs with all the strength I could summon. When I reached the top, he confirmed I was faster than Achilles, and my chest heaved with pride and satisfaction. Nick had said something about "stages" and a "story."

As I exhaled, I was hit with the full memory of the event and the words that had been blurry all those years suddenly became crisp, as if Nick were saying them then and there.

"The stories of the heroes are the stories of each and every one of us as we grow up and move from one stage of life to the next. It's a bit like climbing the terraces," he had said, pointing at the stone steps. "What's important to remember, in the end, is that we're meant to be the hero in our own story."

Nick was smiling at me when our eyes met again. He winked and tapped the roof of the car.

"Let's go."

www.ingramcontent.com/pod-product-compliance
Lightning Source LLC
Chambersburg PA
CBHW051150130726
47988CB00005B/2062